Library of Congress Catalog Card Number 2019941701
ISBN 13: 978-1-941958-95-7/eBook ISBN 978-1-941958-05-6 /
Kindle: 978-1-941958-04-9

For more information, contact queries@cedargrovebooks.com

www.cedargrovebooks.com

Acknowledgements

Thank you, Laura Fasching and Michael Wood, for dealing with my odd timelines – still as strange as they were when we started this thing so many years ago. I also appreciate your candor, though I could throw away your red pens and not feel bad about that at all.

Thank you, Sean and Bree, for giving me time to think when I needed it and for distracting me when that was the better choice.

Thank you, reader, for consuming these words and letting them do what they do.

For SAW, BKW, and MDW… always

THE REALM

Chapter One

It didn't happen the way they said it would.

No angels came to greet him; no bright light funneled a path through the darkness. No relatives called to him from the beyond.

He didn't feel warmth, acceptance, or love – he felt emptiness.

He saw nothing in the moments before death. Just an impenetrable darkness that crowded his vision like oil spreading in water, encroaching on the faces of his son and daughter-in-law, blackening them: obliterating them. He could hear them after his eyes dimmed, standing open and blind like black holes. His tear ducts dried up as his son cried over him.

The sound of Doug's grief, the guttural moans roiling and meshing with his pleas—his barters with God to save his father— was more than Patrick could take. Trying but failing to lift his hand from his side and stroke his son's head, Patrick silently prayed that his hearing would dissipate as quickly as his sight had.

Patrick could only imagine what Doug and Chris were seeing as his body broke down in front of him. Images of eyes ruined by broken capillaries filled with blood, his slacked mouth allowing a discolored tongue to peek through tortured his mind. He struggled for every breath now, death's grip holding fast and firm. The thought of the kids seeing him fight for air, his face a twisted mass of pain and effort, upset him more than he thought it would. Death was not pretty.

Doug moaned and Chris cried while Patrick's eyes grew drier and his skin grew paler. He thought it would never end, the display, the sick, cruel game death was playing. That he should witness it, that he should have to hear the calmness his son usually displayed crumble and fall away, was torture if ever there was a definition of the word. The devil, then. It was his work after all, he supposed. He was on his way to Hell and this was but a taste of what was to come.

And then there was silence.

Utter silence.

The sound of his son's anguish was gone, mercifully. The hum of the respirator, the clicking of the rosary beads the man in the next bed held, the squeak of rubber soles on the sanitized tile floor as the nurses and doctors hurried to his side - all sound had disappeared. He wondered what would be next to go. His memory? He quizzed himself just to see if it was already gone. *What's my name? Patrick Richardson. How old am I? 59. Was is more like it,* he corrected himself. After all, he was dead. Dead. Gone. Finished.

Patrick stood in the pitch-black silence confused and unbelievably sad. He was dead. He would never see the baby that Chris was carrying, his first grandchild. He wouldn't ever watch another boxing match with his son and friends over beer and pizza. He wouldn't get the chance to watch the waves break on the shore from a beach chair in the Caribbean. He wouldn't do anything anymore—not eat, drink, or fuck—ever again. Because he was dead.

And death was dark. Impenetrably so.

How did this happen? he asked aloud using a mouth he could no longer feel. He thought back to that morning, when he was taking out the garbage. He could remember walking to the back of his house and getting the garbage can. The damned cat had gotten into it again; the little stray he left food and water for had knocked the top of the can off, torn through the garbage bag, and gotten to the trash inside. The little monster made a hell of mess too, strewing soggy newspaper, chicken bones, and juice cartons all over the brick patio. Patrick remembered cursing out loud and casting his eyes around the backyard, looking for the cat. He remembered turning back to the bowl he'd left out the night before and finding it full of food. 'That's what you were supposed to eat, damn it!' he'd said as he bent down to clean up the mess.

On his way back into the house to get another garbage bag, a piece of the dream he had the night before came back to him. It hung in front of his eyes like a transparency over real life, framing everything with the hazy film of familiarity, all soft edges and anticipation.

Déjà vu.

As usual after those dreams, the dark ones that made him wonder if he was there, really there, walking, talking, living within them, he wondered if he was the character whose face the audience never sees.

The memory was faint, as it always was the morning after, but he knew what happened next. This time the scene was identical to his dream. There was usually something askew, some crucial piece off center, but this time nothing was out of place. He knew he would turn away from the door instead of going inside to get the garbage bag. He knew he would squint from the sun when he did, and that he would place his hands above his eyes, shading them like a visor. He knew it just as well as he knew his name, for as easily as that knowledge came, it dragged heavy fear and worry in its wake.

He obliged. It wasn't like he had a choice.

Patrick heard a shriek coming from the next door pulling him away from the dream world and into the land of the living with a jolt. It came from Mary Williams' house, an old lady who lived alone despite her diminished vision and limited use of her legs. She got along fine, though. She cooked her own meals and cleaned her own house. She hardly left anything for the day nurse to do. *Spunky old girl*, Patrick remembered thinking. *I hope I'm as "with it" as she is when I get to be that old.* Something cold took up residence in his stomach, grafting itself to his insides and pulsating there.

The shrieking voice didn't sound like Mary's, though. It sounded younger, more vibrant, less gravelly and weathered with age. It was probably the day nurse, Jennifer. With a sigh, Patrick detoured from his front door, crossing his lawn to mount Mary's front steps. *The ole girl might have kicked the bucket*, he thought as he approached the door. He felt genuinely saddened by the idea.

The dream was dissipating, and Patrick was happy about that. Sure, he could still feel it playing along the edges of his consciousness, enticing him to come back to play. But it would lose this time and evermore.

Patrick knocked on the door and called out to Jennifer, Mary's nurse, announcing himself. The door was ajar, and the force of his knuckles pushed it open. Patrick walked inside hesitantly, calling for Jennifer all the while, but there was no response. He called for Mary then, wondering if something had happened to the girl instead. Nothing. Two steps into the foyer and Patrick could see into the living room and dining room on the opposite side of the hallway. There was no one in sight. Patrick remembered thinking he should leave, thinking that he had been hearing things. *But why didn't they answer? And why was the front door open?* That Jennifer's car was in the driveway didn't register in his mind when it happened, but Patrick could remember it as clear as day as he recounted it. If he could do it all over again, he would do the same thing, he was sure of it. What happened was just meant to be.

He went into the living room, intending to walk through to the kitchen and into the family room. If they weren't in there, he would go upstairs and check the bedrooms, then in the backyard. If he still couldn't find them, he would call the police. Mary rarely went out of the house, even with Jennifer's help. She enjoyed sitting in her backyard or in the window facing the road. "Parks can't give me any more scenery than my backyard can," she always said. "And I even get a glimpse of a handsome young man with his shirt off from time to time." Patrick snickered at the thought (at least he thought he did). Him, a handsome young man? Right. Young wasn't a word that was being used to describe him anymore, at least not by the women he dated. Distinguished? Maybe. Vibrant? Sure. Young? No. But he kept himself in shape, enough that he wasn't ashamed to walk around with his shirt off. The sun on his back always felt good to him, ever since he was a kid working in the yard with his dad. And hell, if you looked hard enough, you could almost see his six-pack hiding beneath the layer of skin that stubbornly refused to flatten out. So, if Mary liked to sneak a peek at him, she could go right ahead.

Patrick almost made it through the living room when the shot rang out. The bullet punctured his chest, immobilizing his left arm and driving him to the floor before he could take his next step. He never saw the man who shot him, never saw what he had done to Mary and Jennifer, their bodies tied to dining room chairs that lined the wall of the kitchen, out of view from the picture window in the family room. All he knew was the hot, searing pain in his chest that seemed to burn his insides and the blood that poured from the entry wound to wet his skin with its warmth.

Patrick remembered the feeling of the bullet tearing through his body, seeming to seek out a place to rest, to destroy.

He woke up in the hospital to Doug and Chris's faces, tear-streaked and raw. There was more wrong with him than he thought, he could see it in Doug's eyes. His son, always the cool and collected one, always the optimist. He could find a silver lining in every cloud. But not in this one. This time he saw a rain cloud for what it was, knew the storm was coming and when it was over, nothing would be the better for it.

And then...

Where the hell was Joanne, anyway? Wasn't she supposed to have met him at the pearly gates when he died? Patrick thought bitterly. Doug and Patrick had lost Joanne ten years before to breast cancer. Patrick liked to imagine that she would be there waiting for him when it was his turn. He thought she would come for him, would ease him away from life, his pain dissipating as he looked into her beautiful eyes. That's what they said would happen, those preachers he had listened to and believed over the years since Joanne died – the ones he clung to desperately, needing to believe they knew what they were talking about. So, where was she?

Where was his mother? His father? What about Jennifer and Mary? They were dead too, weren't they? That's what Doug and Chris were talking about when he came to. He remembered hearing his son, his level-headed boy, cursing God for letting his father walk into that house. What about them? Surely, they would come to greet the man who tried to help them, who died because he cared?

But he was alone. In darkness.

Anger coursed through him as he searched the pitch for something, someone. And then, profound sadness overtook him as rapidly and completely as his anger had. His son would raise his child to remember his grandpa instead of actually knowing him. A prayer would be sent up for him on holidays and his birthday for as long as Doug was alive. But after that there wouldn't be anyone left to remember. His would be just another headstone at a cemetery overgrown with weeds; just an old picture in a dusty frame of a man his granddaughter and great-grandchildren would never know. Patrick had ceased to be.

He felt lightheaded.

No, he corrected himself. Lightheaded might be what he would have felt if he were still alive, still in the body that had walked the earth for 59 years. He longed to feel lightheaded - he wanted it so badly that he allowed himself to think it was what he really felt. But, he realized with more poignancy than he would have liked, he didn't feel anything. Nothing at all.

CHAPTER TWO

The darkness faded to light much like it does in the movies. It jarred Patrick's senses, terrified him. He had just gotten used to the darkness, the tangible blackness that had surrounded him since the moment his last breath expelled from his lips into the sterile air of the hospital. He remembered feeling his breath pass over the chapped skin of his lips, remembered knowing he would never draw another one in. He wished he could grab the breath back, hold it in his mouth a second, or two, or three longer. He still did.

But that didn't happen.

Instead, his eyes opened to a new life, a new existence. He could see things, like the room he was in, the color of the tile that covered the floor (light gray with darker gray speckles, the surface of which had been mopped repeatedly making the darker gray fade into the lighter), the people sharing the space with him. He could see them just as clearly as he could when he breathed the same air they did, but he couldn't touch them. Not in any way that was physical. The woman in the room, her sweet perfume filling Patrick's nostrils, making him yearn to touch her, to touch anything, stood at the far end of a table. She wasn't looking at them, not really. She scanned the room, her eyes never resting on anything for longer than a second or two. It was deliberate avoidance and it made Patrick nervous.

Patrick watched her, willing her to meet his eyes. He could see her chest rise and fall as she breathed, her breasts heaving up and down, up and down. She was beautiful. Soft brown hair framed her natural face, devoid of makeup and fresh. The hint of a smile played at the corners of her lips as she worked: the natural pose of her delicate mouth. A beauty. Patrick might have hit on her had he been younger or she been older. Or if he had been alive.

There were three men in the room, one with a clipboard. All three of them had surgical masks resting on their chests, ready to be pulled over their mouths.

Patrick could feel the floor beneath his feet, could actually feel the cool tiles as his bare feet slapped them. His movements were effortless; he barely knew he was making them. He lifted a hand to his face and could see his skin, tanned from a vacation in the Bahamas two weeks before. But how could he see it? He was dead!

"Shall we get started, gentlemen?" The woman pulled her surgical mask over her pretty little mouth and snapped latex gloves over her hands. The guy holding the clipboard pressed RECORD and started speaking into the recorder: "Date: August 29, 2023. Collier, Sampson, and Finch attending. Subject is male, fifty-nine years of age, 5 foot 11 inches, 198 pounds." His voice was robotic, going through Patrick's vitals as though they were just facts. "No distinguishing marks, no rigor." The snap of the STOP button on the recorder was like a firecracker to Patrick's ears.

"Do you want to do the honors, Finch?" The woman nodded encouragingly to the one holding the clipboard. "Thank you, Dr. Collier." He sat the clipboard down and handed the recorder over to her. She pressed the RECORD button and continued: "Dr. Finch will make the Y incision."

Patrick jerked away, ready to get up but the woman touched his shoulder and stilled him. It was warm and comforting. He would have done anything to keep her hand on him, even if he couldn't really feel it. Watching Finch's novice hands cut into his flesh didn't bother Patrick as much as seeing the saw prepared did. Sampson silently checked the plug for the device, tightened the blade, made all the minor adjustments needed for use. Patrick had watched all the medical reality shows on cable; he knew what was coming next. But that didn't make it any easier. Not when it was his body.

The flesh of his torso was incised into the pattern of a Y, the arms extending from either shoulder to meet above his sternum and descend to the stem above his pelvis. The top flap that drew a V beneath his chin was rolled over his face before Patrick got a chance to see himself. It was just as well. He didn't know if he could handle the sight.

Sampson handed the saw to Finch who didn't hesitate to cut through Patrick's ribs, and expose his organs. Patrick squinted through lowered eyelids at his insides. His lungs were gray and deflated, no doubt due to all the smoking he'd done over the past twenty years. "Shit," Patrick whispered. His heart, liver, and stomach all glistened in his blood; streaks of it cooled in the open air. He couldn't believe he was looking inside himself. He couldn't believe he was dead.

"Heart: 272 grams. Liver: 1400 grams…" *Is that good or bad?* Patrick wondered as Finch rattled off the weight of his organs. He noticed Collier leaning over his head, preparing to perform more checks and balances. The flap of skin that had hidden his face from view had been pushed away and the upper half of his face had been pulled down over the bottom half, exposing the top of his skull. A gelatinous substance that made him think of cooling fat covered the underside of his skin, and Patrick immediately wished he hadn't looked. He heard the low hum of the Stryker saw echo off the sterile walls. He turned away when she broke through, wishing he was somewhere else. Her hands cupped his skullcap to remove it and expose his brain.

The doctors fussed over his body, nothing more than a shell left behind, like the hard casing of a peanut after being cracked. And that's what it was, after all. A discarded shell. An empty casing. His body couldn't reanimate, couldn't get up from the table and demand to be stitched back up and sent on its way. It wasn't anything at all anymore.

Patrick looked over his muscular calves and thighs, his package, all from a new perspective. He'd never had the pleasure of seeing himself from that angle before, and it was interesting. The way the tips of his toes leaned toward each other, the shape of his knees, knobby, if not boney, the curve of his muscles. He'd never get the chance to use them again. What he was using then, that ethereal body, if you could call it that, was as light as the air itself. He couldn't feel skin beneath his touch, which made him wonder if the tanned arm he saw was nothing more than a memory, a wish. He sensed that he was occupying space in the same manner as he might have when he lived; the same mass, the same height. He cast a forlorn glance at himself once more, as the doctors chattered about a massive hemothorax that he had suffered and insurmountable post-operative bleeding— it was all blather, to him—, unable to shake the sadness that hovered like a cloud. His pallid skin, tanned on the surface, but devoid of natural color, devoid of life, looked like stone. His innards were splayed on the autopsy table in the open air. He was dead.

It was over.

He turned his back on Drs. Collier, Sampson, and Finch, leaving the room as they started to sew him back up. He didn't need to hear their conclusions about how he died—he knew how it happened. He was there. He didn't need to see what his face looked like after they rolled the skin back over his skull.

CHAPTER THREE

People walked briskly to and fro, passing on either side of him. He couldn't stop staring at a girl who seemed to have looked right at him. *They can see me*, he told himself. He was sure of it. But how?

He had walked out of the coroner's office without incident, wondering all the while what room Joanne had lain in, if she had witnessed her autopsy as well. Had she stood behind the doctors as they cut her open and pulled out her innards to be weighed and measured? She wouldn't have been able to take it. The tiniest drop of blood from a splinter or a paper cut was enough to drive her into hysterics. Seeing herself split in half and splayed? No. She would have left far earlier than he had. If she was there at all. Was he in Hell? Was that why he was subjected to seeing himself in death, made to smell the scent of his own blood? If so, get on with it. Bring out the Devil, the welcoming crew. If he was in Hell, for whatever reason, he would be able to understand why Joanne hadn't come. She couldn't. Surely, she was in Heaven, if anyone was. That had to be it.

Or was it?

What if he was in Heaven and that was all there was, a gauze on the world he used to live in, a haze within which people like him existed? People like him – what did that mean? There wasn't anything special about Patrick, not that he could think of. He ate, drank, shat, and slept like everyone else in the world did – better than some, worse than others. The tenets of Heaven and Hell should apply to him as they had to his wife, as they had for everything that lives. That's what the Bible said (though he hadn't read it in a while, he remembered enough to know the general theme). He should be in one place or the other.

So why did he feel homeless, so utterly alone?

Joanne hadn't been any different than him. She wasn't one of the churchgoing folks that packed their local holy place every Sunday and filled the tithe tray, lining the Pastor's pockets. She believed in God, sure, but she didn't fellowship or evangelize. Hell, he and Joanne weren't sure they knew what that even meant. She wasn't a bad person, not by anyone's stretch of the imagination. She was a volunteer at the hospital and a crossing guard for the grade school. Patrick donated money and clothes to the homeless and even sent money off to sponsor a needy child oversees. They were good people. So, what the hell was going on?

As Patrick walked down the dark hallways of the morgue (the shadows, the unnatural cool frightening him, even then), he couldn't shake the nagging question that rang in his ears, ricocheted in his head. *Where the hell am I?*

When he stepped onto the sidewalk, busy with rush hour foot traffic, he didn't feel the gravel dig into his feet or the gum that would have stuck to a man's foot had he stepped where Patrick did. That didn't strike him as odd anymore – he'd gotten over the shock of being intangible the autopsy room. Almost. It was when the woman, an Asian girl with brown highlights in her jet-black hair and purposeful eyes, looked at him and saw him—really saw him—that his confusion mounted again. He stared after her as she made her way up the street, barely slowing, but hesitating enough for Patrick to notice. She saw him. So did the man that passed on his other side. He was preoccupied; he brushed past Patrick a millisecond after looking down at his watch. He actually flinched when he made contact with Patrick—the expression was faint, barely noticeable. But Patrick saw it.

They were seeing him. Living, breathing people could see him standing among them. *What must I look like?* he wondered. A ghost? Sure. But what did *that* look like? Was he transparent? Silhouetted? Was the appearance of his body reduced? Faded? Muted? So faint, they weren't sure they saw anything at all? Patrick looked down at himself then, suddenly terrified that the image they might have seen, whatever translucence, whatever pitch, might be nude.

It wasn't.

The problem was, he couldn't make out what, if anything, covered him. His legs and feet were hidden from view. He was amorphous, formless, as though a colorless sack covered his body.

Patrick decided to try something that he remembered from a movie. Ghosts were always moving things, tables and chairs mostly, but sometimes more substantial objects. They were always able to make their presence known to people, even though they were dead and gone. He decided he would try to make contact. Patrick needed to know if people could see him, could feel him in some way. If they could, then maybe he wasn't really dead. Maybe it was all a terrible dream, a horrible nightmare, and he was still asleep. Maybe he hadn't gotten up to take the garbage out yet, hadn't gone over to Mary's house, hadn't been shot. Hell, Mary was probably already up and sitting in her back yard waiting for him to flash her some skin. Maybe he was still asleep in his bed. He had almost convinced himself of that when a word, spoken in his own voice, floated back to him, flooding his ears. *Ghost.*

Patrick walked briskly over to the newspaper stand on the corner, trying to ignore the fact that he had walked through people as though they weren't there in the process. The attendant looked past him with weary, watery eyes. Patrick tried to move into the man's line of sight, trying to make the older man see him as the two on the street seemed to have. Nothing. The man just stared ahead, looking at nothing and at everything at the same time, waiting for customers to buy his newspapers and his candy.

Patrick tried speaking, feeling badly before he started. What would he have done if he, all of a sudden, started hearing a disembodied voice speaking to him? It would freak him out, would make him think he had finally lost it. Patrick looked back at the man who looked older than he was, with heavy bags under his eyes, deep lines in his face, and a permanent scowl. His salt and pepper hair was oily; it fell into his weathered face, tanned by the beating of the sun and reddened by the cutting wind. The guy looked out at Patrick, seeing but not seeing, his eyes vacant from the monotony. Patrick hated doing it to the guy, but he had to know.

"Excuse me," he started meekly. "Hello?"

Nothing.

"Can you hear me?"

Nothing.

Patrick got frustrated. Louder, he said, "Old man, can you hear me?"

Nothing.

Patrick sighed, the air seeming to course through him hot and sticky. He rested his hands against the side of the cart, not feeling the cool metal beneath his palms. He tried once more.

"Goddamn it, do you hear me?" His voice boomed loudly on the plane where he stood but fell on deaf ears in the vendor's world. The world Patrick had occupied that morning.

The reality of his death set upon him like a storm cloud releasing its fury overhead.

Like a sheet being pulled over his head.

Infuriated, Patrick tried to pick up a candy bar and wave it in front of the man's face. He couldn't do it. He looked down at his hands and found he could see the candy bars and mints lined up in neat rows through them. He could even see the newspapers below and the ground beneath them. Patrick lashed out, trying his hardest to knock over the candy, to ruffle the newspapers, to make any impact at all.

Nothing.

"Fuck!" he yelled, his voice full of despair and anguish, and silent to everyone else around him.

CHAPTER FOUR

"They can only see you if they're on the way out."

The voice came from out of nowhere and from all around him at the same time. Patrick was startled and he jumped even though the notion of such seemed ridiculous to him. *Whoever it is, they can't hurt me,* he told himself, *I'm already dead.*

"What?" Patrick questioned aloud, his voice betraying his nervousness.

"They can't see you unless they are dying themselves." Patrick searched around him, scanning the busy city street, staring at the passersby who were oblivious to him. He couldn't figure out who was speaking to him. "Imminently, of course," the male voice, youngish and inherently pessimistic, continued. "After all, they are all dying, aren't they?"

"Who are you? Show yourself."

"I'm right in front of you, Patrick."

Patrick had the distinct feeling that he was beginning to sweat, though he knew it couldn't possibly be true. The memory of his uncle despairing over the itch in his amputated leg came to mind and he quickly stamped it out.

"I don't see you." He searched, whipping his head to and fro. "I don't see you," he repeated, his voice taking on a panicked edge.

There.

The man was young, just like he sounded. Probably only in his late twenties. His hair was oily and long, he had a perpetual smirk. He was amused at my nervousness not overly so. He'd seen it all before.

He wasn't lying either. He was standing right in front of Patrick.

Patrick jumped and lurched backward, putting distance between the man and himself. The man smiled at Patrick's reaction and chewed the inside of his cheek, working his lips like he would around the butt of a cigarette. He was dressed in a uniform; blue on blue. His short-sleeves were rolled up and the shirt showed considerable wear exactly where a cigarette would have been held. He was cool in a James Dean kind of way and, apparently, was like him in other ways as well.

"It's always the same when you first get here. I know. I went through it too."

"Here? Where is here?" Patrick asked, bewildered.

"The anger, the disbelief," the man continued. "I asked a guy on the street if he could see me too, tried to push him down when he didn't respond. I was sure he could see me, could hear me talking to him. He looked right at me."

Patrick nodded, helpless to do anything else.

"But I fell right through him when I tried to push him. And he kept walking, shaking me off like a cool breeze." The man snickered and ran a hand through his heavy hair.

"What is this? Where are we?"

"They can't see you, unless they are about to die," the man said again, ignoring Patrick's questions. "Some of them can, but it's rare to find them. It's usually only the ones that are on their way out who can see you, and even they don't see you clearly all the time. But the ones that do," he shook his head, "it's freaky, man. Go to the hospital and stand next to the bed of a terminal patient, one that doesn't have more than a day or so to live. They fucking talk to you, man! They can hear you and see you, like you're alive."

Patrick shook his head, trying to clear it.

"I tried it out, you know? Went to the burn unit of the hospital they had my body in. Walked in on an old guy who got trapped in his apartment building while it burned around him. There was no way he was gonna make it. He was hooked up to a million machines, all beeping and hissing with his every breath. I walked into the room and stood over him, mute. I didn't say a thing. I couldn't think of anything *to* say. I didn't know why I was there, except that I was supposed to be." The guy looked past Patrick at something: a memory floating in the distance. "So, I stood over this guy and he opened his eyes and looked at me. Asked me if I was there to take him back with me. I couldn't answer him. I didn't know what to say. And the man looked so at peace when he saw me, so comfortable. I couldn't handle it, so I walked out of the room."

He chewed on the inside of his cheek some more.

"Where the hell are we?"

"We're where we are. Where we go after we die. This is it buddy. No pearly gates, no angels with wings. Just this." Patrick looked away from the man and cast his eyes around them, letting them fall on the opaque world he was encased within.

"No," Patrick said, his voice cracking. "It can't be."

"Ain't much, huh?" The man pursed his lips like he wanted to spit a wad of tobacco onto the ground. A wad he didn't have.

"But why?"

The man sighed and said, "Hey look, if you don't believe me check it out for yourself. The pretty young girl that saw you will die tonight in her bed. The guy that passed you, the one looking at his watch, he doesn't even have that long. Follow him to the subway and he'll prove my point before he makes it to the platform."

Patrick's face was blank, void of emotion, as he watched the living pass by.

"Go to the hospital, talk to one of the people in there dying," the man continued. "You'll see what I mean."

Patrick barely heard him talking.

"Patrick?"

He didn't answer. He didn't even turn in the man's direction. It didn't register to him that some long dead guy just spoke his name as if he'd known Patrick for years.

"See for yourself."

The man did spit then, a puff of air spewing from his mouth. He backed away, turning only after stepping several paces backward. Before he walked away, he added, "If you find one that can see you and doesn't die soon after, run like hell."

Patrick turned around in time to see the man disappear in the crowd of people.

CHAPTER FIVE

Patrick walked in a daze toward the subway, his feet moving of their own volition. He knew the man was watching him, walking with him was there somewhere among the crowd. Patrick didn't try to look for him; he didn't want to see him. Doing so again would make the whole thing real.

The steps leading to the subway were steep and dark: only the tops of them stood out, protruding in the light like a tongue inside a gapping mouth. It was cavernous, daunting. Patrick had never liked subway stations, their stairwells leading into the ground beneath the world people lived in and into the bowels of the earth. He always felt like he was stepping into Hell whenever he used them. Patrick stared into the abyss, lost in his own thoughts, when the man who had passed him on the corner brushed by him again.

Patrick watched as the man started down the steps with irritation written all over his face. He looked at his watch once, twice, three times. He must be late for something, Patrick guessed, regretting the time he'd spent rushing to and from the office. Patrick started after him, quickening his pace to catch up to the man. There didn't seem to be anything wrong with him. He was fit with an athletic build with just the slightest hint of gray forming at his temples. He looked to be in perfect health and moved like it. Patrick was sure the man who prophesized his death had been wrong.

He closed the space between them, stepping close enough to touch him. Patrick couldn't help but stare at him, to read his face, trying to see if any concept of his presence had resonated. As Patrick watched the man's face twisted into a grimace, not a full-fledged, teeth bared, snarl, but a tight-lipped one. His free hand clutched at some invisible ball beneath his skin, underneath his ribs as he slowed to a stop on the stairs. Commuters walked up and down the darkened stairs, oblivious to the man's pain. Patrick watched in horror as the man fell to the landing, falling head over foot on the stairs, and spilling the contents of his briefcase onto the dingy platform.

Patrick raced toward him, feeling himself lift from the ground in his urgency. He kneeled next to the man and asked,

"Son, can you see me?"

The man, open mouthed, red faced, and in shock, said weakly, "Yes-"

"Don't try to talk," Patrick said, knowing that it didn't matter if he did or didn't.

"Help me," the man on the landing begged, tears streaming from his eyes and rolling down the side of his face to wet the hair at his temples.

Patrick couldn't console him, this stranger he had only followed to satisfy his own curiosity. He felt selfish and ashamed of himself.

Patrick looked at the man's dying eyes, seeing what he imagined his son must have seen as he sat next to his deathbed. He could feel the man tugging at him, needing to connect.

"Just rest, son. It'll all be over soon."

Patrick stood up and watched the people rush toward the man who lay dying on the subway landing. There were shrieks of horror and people calling for the police. Patrick could hear the chatter of the people in the back of the group, the ones who couldn't see what was going on, asking: 'What the hell is going on up there?' 'What, did somebody get mugged?' 'Jesus, can't you move it to the side? Some of us have jobs to go to.'

He didn't have to look hard to find the man who predicted it all. He was sitting on the top step of the subway entrance, chewing his cheek absently like he had been before. A woman walked through him to descend the steps. He didn't flinch.

"You better get used to that. It happens all the time."

Patrick couldn't get the dying man's face out of his head.

"How'd it happen?" Patrick asked, stricken. "What killed him? He looked fine!"

"Well so did you, but you're still dead, aren't you?"

"Yeah, but –."

"What does it matter anyway? Dead is dead, right? Heart attack killed this poor sap, but if his great-great-great grandfather hadn't passed heart disease down the family chain, the train would have hit him at that very instant. You get me?"

Patrick didn't. He didn't get any of it.

"He was supposed to die right then. That minute, that second. It's written."

"Fate? Are you saying God knows the exact moment we're going to die?"

He reclined on the step and propped his arms on the gravel. "You better drop all that religious mumbo jumbo you learned growing up. It ain't gonna help you here."

Patrick turned around and looked down the stairs. The crowd still surrounded the man, encircling him as he lay on the cold concrete.

Turning back to the stoic man was like shutting his eyes against reality and opening them in a fantasy. "So, what are you saying? If not God, then who?"

The man looked uncomfortable. He stood and mounted the top stair, walking away from the subway.

Patrick followed behind him quickly, shouting, "Hey, wait a minute! What's the hurry? I mean," he said ruefully, "we don't have anywhere to go, do we?"

The man, not more than a kid, really, looked at him with an emotion in his eyes that Patrick couldn't place. "What's your name anyway?" Patrick asked to break the silence.

"Mark." His voice was as low as a whisper.

"I'm Patrick."

"I know," he said, turning toward the older man, a smile playing at the corners of his mouth.

"How can you know that? How do you know things and I don't?" Patrick asked, his brow furrowed.

"You do know them. You just haven't opened yourself to it yet."

"To what?"

"To this," he said, stretching his arms to either side and gesturing around them. "All of it. This world, this existence."

Patrick looked at the haze that covered the city street. He stared through it, focusing on the sidewalk, on the stones lodged in the cement. The haze dissipated a little, as though he had driven through a fog and was emerging in the clear day on the other side.

"You have to let go of the world you left and embrace this one before you can see what I see, before your mind will allow you to accept the things you already know in your heart. I'm not telling you to forget. You'll never do that. But I'm telling you to accept that you're here, that you're one of us. That you're not one of them. Not anymore."

The sidewalk cleared more and more as Patrick focused on it. A bone colored pebble first, its worn shaped sides and smooth surface coming into view where it had been nothing more than a shadow before. But still, the haze was present.

"Where *is* here, Mark? What are we? Ghosts? Spirits? Souls? What?"

Something flashed hot behind Mark's eyes. A mixture of a snarl and a smile mingled on his face as he pursed his lips to spit again.

Finally, after what seemed like an eternity, he said, "We're his."

CHAPTER SIX

'We're his,' Mark said. Whose? Patrick tried asking, but Mark ignored the question and kept walking. Patrick turned around after a lengthy silence, during which the man on the platform drifted up from the darkened corridor of the subway station and passed them. The man was confused. He looked around himself incredulously, as if seeing the street for the very first time. Patrick supposed that was close to the truth. Patrick made hesitant eye contact with the bewildered man. His eyes registered recognition and for a moment Patrick thought the man might speak to him. But he didn't. Instead, he retreated, stumbled away, put as much distance between himself and Patrick as he could.

He recognized Patrick.

And it terrified him.

Mark's pace quickened and Patrick raced to catch up. "Where are we heading?"

Mark was silent.

"Look, what the hell is all of this about?" Patrick said, more than a little frustrated. "Why all the secrecy?"

"You'll see where we're going when we get there."

Intrigued, Patrick settled into a steady gait alongside Mark. He looked at him from the corner of his eye. Mark was of slight build, skinny almost. His long black hair looked unkempt; his skin sallow. Specks of dirt dotted his face and forearms; he looked in need of a bath. Patrick almost laughed out loud at the absurdity of his thoughts.

"How long did it take me to get up and walk away from my body after I... died? It couldn't have been more than five minutes since that guy died."

"About the same as him, but it was much longer than 5 minutes. Time isn't the same. It goes by faster. What would have been hours when we were alive are only minutes here. Look around you."

Patrick hadn't noticed the sky darkening and the street traffic clearing out. He had been engrossed in conversation. How long had it been? Five? Ten minutes? An entire day had passed in that span of time.

"My God," Patrick said, his voice almost a whisper.

"There are other things too. Everything is different here. But you'll find that out later."

Patrick and Mark walked in silence the rest of the way. Patrick tried to take in everything around him, the shadow of the buildings, the street, the closed businesses. He tried to feel the breeze on his cheeks, knowing he wouldn't.

They turned onto a street Patrick remembered—Waters Lane. Most of the businesses were closed down and had been for ten years. But the funeral home was still open. Most of Patrick's family had been prepared and eulogized there, as far back as his great-grandfather. All of his siblings and their families had used them. Patrick had been there so many times, he knew the decoration patterns of each of the seven viewing rooms.

Mark stopped at the entrance to the United Funeral Home and looked at Patrick who stood paces away from the door. "You have to do this," Mark said, his voice grave. "It's the only way to move on."

Patrick took a deep breath and thought of walking through the threshold. Images of his previous visits flooded his mind, bringing clothes for his uncle to be dressed in; hosting the wake for his father; selecting a casket for Joanne. So much sorrow, so much pain. He felt it weighing down on him, pressing on his shoulders, crushing his chest. The feeling was debilitating.

"I don't think I can do it," Patrick said meekly. "I don't think I can go inside."

Mark placed a hand on his shoulder. Patrick was surprised he could feel the reassuring touch. "You have to," he said firmly. "It's the only way."

Patrick stared at the door, oblivious to the sky's early morning blue creeping in to overtake the night. The ornate lettering on the door to the funeral parlor had always fascinated him. He loved the calligraphy, the elaborate loops and embellishments. He stared at it, trying to calm his nerves, but it didn't work. How do you calm down before seeing your own dead body? Taking a deep breath, Patrick pushed open the door and went inside.

The sign near the door directed mourners to viewing room #2 to view Patrick's body before the ceremony. Patrick could feel his stomach drop as he read the sign: Viewing room #2. Jesus.

Patrick entered the room slowly, not eager to stand before his body laid out in a casket. He and his college buddies used to kick the concept of life after death around all the time. They challenged the doctrines of religion, the Catholic Church, the reasons why there were so many facets of Christianity, God or Jehovah, or Buddha, or Allah. They cracked open the Bible on many occasions to decipher the true meaning of it and how it applied in the modern-day world. They thought they were enlightened, thought they had figured the whole

36

thing out. But standing over his casket, Patrick knew they hadn't even scratched the surface. Everything they had discussed had been turned on its ear the moment Patrick stood up from his deathbed.

Doug had put him in his best blue suit. Canary yellow shirt, navy and red tie, sparkling cuff links. He couldn't have done better himself. The casket was stately: reddish-brown mahogany with cream lining. *Always thinking ahead*, Patrick thought. Bugs used to be Doug's thing when he was little, before he gave them up for economics and number crunching. He used to capture fireflies and raise ant farms. Patrick and Joanne indulged him, urged him to learn everything he could about them. A fragment of a memory came back to Patrick as he admired the casket's finish: Mahogany is resistant to termites and rot. *Good job, son.*

Patrick was afraid, but he had to look. He had to see for himself if he was every going to let his old life go.

He had a fresh shave. His hair, brown with the beginnings of gray streaking the front like highlights, was neatly trimmed and in place. His eyes were closed, the wrinkles that bunched at the corners were pulled taut, unnaturally so. His lips were pressed together, pouty almost. His face was like a statue – like cold, lifeless stone.

Patrick's eyes cascaded over his chest, unmoving and solid, like a rock, and then down to his stomach, just visible above the closed lower half of the casket. His arms were bent at the elbow; his forearms rested on his stomach and his hands clasped above his belly button. His hands were flat, his fingers folded tightly together. Patrick began to wonder if, in fact, they were laced together, sutured, given their appearance.

Patrick looked away from his body, lying dead in the casket. He suddenly felt sick to his stomach.

As Patrick turned to face the door, he noticed the bouquets of flowers on stands and on the floor. Roses, Carnations, Lilies. All the flowers that provoked memories of death for him when he was alive. He shook his head, realizing they would probably sing 'Amazing

Grace' over his body too. Somehow that made everything more real to him.

Doug and Chris came into the viewing room, startling Patrick. They moved slowly up the aisle, making a concerted effort to keep their composure. Chris's hand was on Doug's back, rubbing soothing circles between his shoulder blades. Usually Chris wore full makeup just to go to the supermarket: mascara and eyeliner, blush, lipstick. But Patrick saw that she only had lip-gloss on. Her dark dress and the bags under her eyes made her look like a much older woman.

Doug was dressed in a suit similar to the one Patrick wore. He had dark, heavy bags beneath his eyes too and his nostrils were rubbed raw. His eyes were wet and glassy. His lips quivered with every step he took.

Patrick wanted to hug his son, to hold him and tell him everything was all right. He couldn't bear to see him in so much pain. He looked for Mark, wanting to leave, but he was nowhere in sight.

Doug approached the casket on legs that were unsteady. Chris fussed with the flowers, straightening the note cards attached, fluffing leaves: trying to find something to do. Doug bent over his father and straightened his tie. The straight face he had been working so hard to keep crumbled as his hand hovered over his father's face. He let the tears come, placing his hand on Patrick's cheek and sobbing into his chest.

Patrick cried with his son. For his son.

"Dad, I miss you so much," Doug whispered.

"I miss you too, Doug. I love you, son." He wished he'd had the chance to say that to him one last time.

"Are you ready?"

Patrick jumped at the sound of Mark's voice. He turned to him and asked, "How can I feel? How can I cry?"

"You only think you're crying. Your face is as dry as mine."

Patrick put a hand to his face and felt nothing.

"Are you ready to move on?"

Patrick turned to look at Doug once more. "Will I ever see him again?" he asked without turning away from the boy who meant the world to him.

"You can see him whenever you choose to for the rest of his life," Mark said, with sadness in his voice.

Chris joined Doug at Patrick's casket and cried with her husband. Patrick nodded, kissing them goodbye in his mind, hoping that in some way, they were able to feel it.

CHAPTER SEVEN

"What happens now?" Patrick asked as they emerged from the funeral home and onto the sidewalk. "Do we roam around down here or do we go up to Heaven?"

"What about Hell?" Mark said. "Isn't it possible that we're going there instead?"

Patrick had had enough. Sure, maybe he was going to Hell. Was that what all this was about? Was all of it designed to break him down before he burned in Hell for eternity? He couldn't image how Hell could be worse than what he had endured. Seeing his son's grief was torture enough.

"Cut the crap, Mark. What happens next? Take me to Hell if that's what you have to do, but do something."

For the first time, Mark's smile was genuine. "Heaven and Hell don't exist the way we thought they did when we were alive. There is a Heaven and a Hell, but they intermingle. They exist on the same plane, in the same space as the living does."

"I don't understand." Patrick couldn't erase the sound of his son's anguish. It was deafening.

"There's no up or down. It's all right here. We walk among the living and they walk among us in The Realm."

"The Realm?" Patrick asked. "What is The Realm?"

"It's everything and nothing. It's here, where the dead inhabit space and time and there," Mark gestured toward a little girl skipping on the sidewalk with her mother trailing behind her, "where the living eat, breath, and sleep. We are all connected. Death is like stepping through a door and into a new room, only that door locks behind you."

Patrick's grandmother used to tell him stories about seeing ghosts and shadows all the time. She swore she saw her mother standing in the backyard near where she was buried. She even claimed that her mother gave her a glass of water on her sick bed. Patrick had always disregarded the stories as fantasy: the ramblings of a lonely old woman. He couldn't have been more wrong.

"How can that be?" Patrick asked, defeated.

"It just is."

"So, if you're bound for hell but you can mingle with the do-gooders, what's the point of it all?" He didn't ask where Joanne was, but he wondered.

"It's not that easy. It may seem open, but it's not. There are boundaries that can't be crossed. We are separated by groups. There are the ones who are in what you think of as Heave and Hell. There are also ones in limbo—."

"Sounds a lot like what the Catholic church talks about to me. Heaven, Hell, Purgatory," Patrick said, anxious for clarity, for meaning.

Mark nodded and said, "But not quite. There are other groups, ones that were never mentioned in anything I have ever seen, and I've read about a lot of religions." Patrick looked at Mark again, taking in the faded tattoo of a dragon on the right side of his neck and found it difficult to believe him.

Mark fell silent, letting Patrick's mind wander. Inexplicably his anger toward Joanne was mounting. He couldn't stop thinking that if she was in the same group he was in, she didn't care about finding him. Could she have found another man here in whatever place they had ended up? Was such a thing possible? He chastised himself for being jealous, for feeling slighted. But old habits die hard.

"The questions you have mulling around in your head will be answered soon enough, though I'm not sure you'll like the answers. I can answer the questions about me right now. I died young – I was only twenty-seven. I took a bad trip and pitched my motorcycle off the side of a cliff. I was raised Catholic, dated a girl who was Muslim, and studied Buddhism before I died. I wasn't any more prepared for what happens in the after life than you were, for all my studying. There's a lot to take in, so you might as well clear your mind of your questions now. Anything else?"

What the hell? We're all mind readers now?

"Did you commit suicide?"

"Yes," Mark said with more than a hint of yearning.

Mark's answer blew Patrick's mind. He had always been taught that people who committed suicide were condemned. Damned to Hell. How could Mark be there? Unless...

"You assume you're in Heaven. That's interesting. Most people think they are already in Hell."

"How can you read my mind? How is that possible?" Enough already.

"Because your mind is open, vulnerable. Your thoughts are like words written on a page for the one who cares to look. It won't always be this way, but it will for a while." Mark chewed the inside of cheek, letting his words sink in. Patrick stared back at him with baleful eyes.

"You're not in Heaven or Hell or Purgatory yet," Mark continued, "you're just... here. It's like being in the foyer of a house: you're there but you haven't gotten into the heart of it yet. And there are many rooms in this house, Patrick. Many more than you think."

Patrick's face softened as he absorbed Mark's words. He watched as people like him walked purposefully among the living, opaque, slightly iridescent beings floating in and out of living beings like cars in traffic.

"Anymore questions?" Mark asked.

"Where is my wife?" He couldn't hold it any longer.

"Your wife is in one of the other groups. She's not ignoring you. She just can't get to you. She's not allowed to."

Patrick hated that his thoughts were so open, so easy for Mark to see. He felt violated.

"Does she know I'm here?"

Mark nodded and looked out into the distance. Hoping that maybe Mark was looking at Joanne, he craned his neck to see, but he didn't see her.

"She heard your son crying."

The whole thing was too much for Patrick to take in. He looked down at the concrete beneath his feet, trying to focus his thoughts.

"Patrick, I know this is a lot, but you have to know it. You have to know where you fit in."

"Where *do* I fit in?" Patrick said, jerking his head up and speaking louder than he intended to. "None of this makes any sense to me."

"And it won't, not for a while. But soon you'll come to understand it." Mark started walking and Patrick stepped in stride next to him. "You are in a group I haven't mentioned yet. You are in the Hunted group."

"The Hunted group?"

"It's for people who died before their time."

Anger shot through Patrick like lightening. "Before their time? How can anyone die before their time? I thought God was supposed to know when we were supposed to die. It's fate. 'Before your time' is nothing more than something we say when someone dies young."

"The group is for people who were killed, and…" Mark hesitated, understanding the full weight of what he was saying, "it's for the people that were turned into killers by someone or something in their life."

Patrick fell silent. Though he knew he had been shot, knew he had died from that wound, it was hard to hear about himself discussed in the context of being murdered.

"I told you, not everything we were taught was true. Like God. You keep talking about what God is supposed to do and what God knows. But there is no God, not in the way that you think. Likewise, there's no Devil like the one we've been told to fear. There isn't some being pulling strings, controlling people like puppets and casting them out if they don't do what He tells them to. He didn't create us in His likeness, though he did create others as such. He gave us free will and watched to see what we did with it. Maybe He won't be as free-wielding with the next batch."

It all sounded like gibberish to Patrick, like some foreign language being shouted at him from different people with varying pitches and inflections in their voices. He remained silent mostly because he couldn't formulate an intelligible question.

"The fallen angel, Satan, Belial, and other names you have probably never heard him called has certain groups under his control," Mark continued. "God does too. And as you'd expect, God is in charge of the ones who go to Arcadia, which is what Heaven is really called. He is also in charge of what you have been taught to call Purgatory, but is actually called, Atonement. He urges the people there to make amends, to repent. Once he's satisfied, he moves them to Arcadia.

"Satan is in charge of those who indulged in sinful acts without remorse: your murders and your rapists. He tries to tempt those in Atonement, but rarely gets anywhere. Those in Atonement are in a unique position to be able to see both Arcadia and Abaddon, which is Hell. They can look into these worlds as easily as if they were looking through a window. Except for some name changes, things are pretty close to what we learned about, right?"

Patrick could do nothing more than nod.

"Here's where things get crazy. There is another player that has never been mentioned in any religious text I have read or heard about. His true name is Mal, but I have also heard him called "The One Who Hunts". He is in charge of the Hunters."

Patrick finally found his tongue and said, "Mark, what are you talking about? I've never heard of anything like this!"

"Neither had I. But I've seen them. I know what they do. You especially want to avoid them at all costs."

A chill ran down Patrick's spine. He tried to tell himself he wasn't really feeling it, but that didn't make the feeling go away.

"Why do I need to avoid them?"

"Because you belong to the Hunted. The murdered ones. You are prey. Those in the Hunted group are not in the Book of Life. That you and others like you ever lived at all was a mistake. The Hunted are homeless, foundationless. Because of that, God doesn't see them. The way that you would die was as invisible to God as the sun to a blind man. Satan doesn't see you either. But Mal does, and he can do whatever he wants with you because you are under the radar. That's why other groups aren't allowed to talk to you, can't even see you in most cases. The Hunted belong to Mal to use for whatever he wants: as food, as a slave, a minion, a sacrifice. For the Hunted, like those suffering in Abaddon, death is only the beginning."

CHAPTER EIGHT

Patrick felt weak. Why was this happening to him? How could it be true that he was never supposed to have been born, was never supposed to exist? He had to ask.

"How does someone just not show up in the Book of Life?"

Mark sighed and chewed the inside of his mouth, a tick he hadn't been able to shed, even in death. "The sins of the father. An ancestor of yours displeased God so much, that he struck him and all his decedents from the Book, cursing them to be born and die without salvation of the soul."

The immensity of Mark's words made Patrick stagger. He thought of Doug and felt like he might pass out.

"Is this irreversible? Are we all damned to this fate?"

"All of those who do not impress Him with their devotion, their love, and even then they will first go to Atonement. Just living a good life will get your line nowhere. They will be preyed upon until the line peters out." Patrick thought about his relatives and tried to make sense of what was he was being told. His mother had died of ovarian cancer, his father in a car accident. His father's father had been pushed out of a window, his great-grandfather had been found with his throat cut. All of them had been involved in shady things, things he didn't know about. Anyone one of them could have brought this curse down on their heads. On Doug's head. He wanted to know who had done this to them more than anything.

"Do you know which of my ancestors did it? I want to meet the bastard." Patrick was angrier than he ever remembered being.

"I don't know who it is, but he or she is, more than likely, in Abaddon. Cast down for the reasons that damn your line. The Hunted can't talk to those in Abaddon. Mal and Satan have agreed to stay out of each other's way. Those in Abaddon are as blind to the Hunters as the Arcadians are, as the living are to everyone in The Realm."

Mark regarded Patrick for a long time before he decided to leave. Chewing the inside of his cheek, he started t walk away. Panic surged within Patrick as he watched Mark pull away.

"Mark, wait. What do I do now?"

Mark was quiet for a long time, keeping his back to Patrick as he stood in silence. Patrick started to speak again but could think of nothing to say. To tell Mark that he was confused would be repetitious. To tell him that he was scared would be stating the obvious. All he knew was he didn't want to be left alone. In The Realm.

Mark turned to face Patrick and regarded him with eyes filled with compassion. When Mark finally spoke, his voice sounded far away. His face, his whole body, seemed to fade into the translucence around them, fading at a fine gradient by the second. "You survive," he said before turning around and walking away, seeming to fall in line with the other oddly iridescent beings that traversed the sidewalk.

CHAPTER NINE

Patrick stood rooted in place for a long time, but Mark didn't come back. Patrick was alone in The Realm. And he was afraid.

The iridescent bodies, like Hollywood aliens in the distance, continued to walk a steady path back and forth on the sidewalk. Patrick decided to join them, to follow the crowd and see where they took him. Though it frightened him to get close to the beings—he hadn't noticed Mark having an iridescent tone, but he supposed he did—he knew he had to. After all, he was one of them.

Patrick joined in step next to an old woman. For the first time, he noticed their nakedness. Everyone was nude. He looked at himself and found that he too was naked. Instinctively, he put a hand over his genitals in an effort to conceal himself in front of the old woman. He wasn't naked before, but the indiscernible cover was gone. If it was ever there at all. He imagined that his skin had flushed bright red, though he couldn't feel the heat welling in his cheeks.

The old woman turned to Patrick and smiled before saying, "There's no need for that, young man. Not anymore."

"I'm sorry," Patrick said quickly. "I'm new." He laughed at how silly he sounded.

"I've been here a long time, though I'm not quite sure how long it's been. You get used to it, the passing of time. Even the nudity becomes commonplace. After a while you don't see it at all."

Patrick found that hard to believe. Though he tried not to, he couldn't help but look at the woman's body, the skin on her face, neck, and above her bosom wrinkled and drawn. Her eyes were watery and sunken; her hair was a halo of bluish gray. Her shoulders were hunched with age and her spine was bent ever so slightly, humped.

"I'm a sight, I know. This is what long life does to you. It destroys the body, deforms it. I barely recognized myself my last ten years. But you never got that far, did you?" Her voice was filled with sorrow. Patrick looked away, longing for all that he had left behind.

"But my husband doesn't see me that way. In his eyes, I look the way I did when we dated; I am his wife from his fondest memories. That's how it is here. The person you know will remain the way they are in your memory, and vice versa. The person you just meet can only look as they did when they died. Which, for you, wasn't too bad at all."

Patrick tried to ignore the fact that he was being paid a compliment by a woman who might have died before he was born.

Patrick looked at the other people walking along the street. Up close, the iridescence wasn't as obvious. In fact, he could barely see it at all. Close up, their translucence filled and they looked like regular people. But they weren't. They were dead. All of them.

"You're getting better already. It won't take long before you see everything The Realm has to offer," the old woman said with a smile on her face.

Patrick looked at her, surprised. How could she know of his progress?

"Do you know me?" Patrick asked.

"Yes." The woman beamed.

"How?

"I am your great-great grandmother on your mother's side. Millicent Nichols?" Patrick tried to remember if he'd heard the name, but he couldn't recall.

"I picked you out myself and sent you down to Gabrielle." Patrick had stopped walking but didn't realize it. Millicent stepped out of the line of the moving dead to talk with her great-great grandson. "You were such a beautiful soul. I knew Gabrielle would be pleased."

"You sent me to my mother? I've been here before?" Patrick was more confused than before.

"We all start in The Realm. We wait for bodies to get into; women who are about to become pregnant."

Patrick looked at Millicent, at her eyes and nose, her smile that was as beautiful as a sunburst, and remembered. Her mother used to tell him the history of his family as she had been told. There wasn't much, just anecdotes here and there about random people, but Patrick remembered one about Millicent. His mother had a favorite brush, one that she only used on special occasions. It had been Millicent's, passed down through her mother.

"You mother used that brush until she died," Millicent said, giving voice to the memory. "She was upset that she didn't have a girl to pass it on to. She saved it, hoping you would have a girl, but you didn't. There won't be a girl in your line for decades yet."

Patrick looked at the woman in a mixture of disbelief and happiness. To connect with someone, to find someone that knew him, loved him, was overwhelming. He hugged the old woman and she returned it with a joyous giggle that made his heart warm.

"Grandmother Millicent, I'm so glad I found you," Patrick said genuinely.

"You would have found one of us, no matter what. We have been walking around on this sidewalk waiting for you to come over." She smiled broad again. "I'm just glad it was me."

Patrick's face turned grave. "Are you part of the Hunted too?"

Millicent gave Patrick a reassuring pat on the cheek. "No, I'm an Arcadian." She gestured back at the people walking on the sidewalk. "We all are."

Patrick's brow furrowed. "I thought Arcadians and Adabbonians couldn't see people like me."

"What Mark told you is mostly true. After you leave, I won't be able to see you either. Only the Hunted and the Hunters will. But when a person dies, the family can come out to greet them and help them understand the lay of the land, so to speak. We are only given a little while to do this, and after that, we have to return to our part of The Realm. Sometimes that means we all go together. But not all the time. You will have to go and be with The Hunted and we will go back to Arcadia."

Patrick shook his head. He didn't want to ask the question in his head, but he needed to hear the answer.

"Will we ever see each other again?"

Millicent's face crumbled and she lowered her eyelids. "No, Patrick, we won't."

Patrick put his arms around Millicent, the woman who had selected him for his mother, a woman he had never known before that day. Had he been able to cry, he would have.

Millicent pulled away and looked over to the sidewalk. She motioned for one of the people there to come over. While they walked, Patrick asked, "Who is Mark? He was the first one to help me."

"Mark is your brother."

Patrick frowned. "I don't have a brother. I was an only child."

Millicent pursed her lips and shook her head. "You have been reunited in The Realm."

Patrick's mouth was still open when his mother spoke. "There are so many things you won't understand, Patrick, not at first," she said softly, almost apologetically. "And I won't be there to explain any of them. I'm sorry."

Patrick turned to his mother. She was as beautiful now as she was in his memories. Her hair was long, hanging just below the shoulders. Her eyes sparkled like they did when he was a kid. She looked young; she looked like she couldn't have been older than 30.she looked as if she was only thirty years old. He hadn't realized that was his favorite memory of her. Patrick was happy to see her that way again, instead of the way she had died – sick old, and tired. "Mom," Patrick said before hugging her tightly. It had been years—fifteen maybe. Too long.

"Patrick," she said, her voice thick and sorrowful. "It's too soon. You shouldn't be here yet. This is wrong."

"Mom," Patrick's heart felt like it was bleeding. "It's ok. There's nothing that could have been done to prevent it. There's some… curse, or something from the family-"

"Your father," she said with sadness thickening her voice. "He's there, in Abbadon. He'll be able to help you." She put her hands on his cheeks and looked at him, soaking him up. Patrick wondered how she saw him, what her favorite memory was. He wanted to ask, but sensed he was running out of time.

"Why didn't Mark tell me?" he asked instead.

"He knew you didn't know about him. He didn't want to be the one to break the news. When he found out about your death, he wanted to be the one to help you through the first stage. He told you more than any of us were told when we got here."

Patrick nodded. He looked into his mother's sorrowful eyes and wanted to stay with her. With Millicent. With Mark, and all the others. But he couldn't. Thoughts of Joanne burned in his mind.

Patrick felt hot suddenly, his temperature creeping up from room temperature to boiling rapidly. His mother cringed as her hands began to burn; smoke drifted up from the place where her palms and his cheeks met.

"Gabrielle, it's time to go," Millicent admonished. "We can't stay any longer."

Patrick's mother nodded and pulled her hands away from his face with concerted effort.

"What's happening, Mom?" Patrick felt panicked.

"We have to go. Our time with you is over." She looked at her hands, at the blisters forming on her palms.

"Does it hurt? Can you feel pain even after death?" Patrick asked.

His mother smiled weakly and said, "It will be gone as soon as I leave you."

Millicent touched Patrick's forearm, pulling her hand back as soon as she contacted his skin, as though she had been stung. "I'm sorry, child," she said quietly. She pulled Gabrielle's arm and repeated, "It's time, honey."

Gabrielle let herself be led a couple of steps backward as she looked at her son's face. Patrick could see the anguish his mother felt and was sure she could see the same in him. It hurt just as much to say goodbye the second time. "I love you, mom," Patrick said.

Gabrielle shrugged off Millicent's hold and ran to her son. She pressed her lips to his cheek, ignoring the sound of her flesh burning as she did it. "I love you," she whispered, choking on emotion.

Patrick kept eye contact with her until his mother and Millicent merged in with the rest of his family on the sidewalk. The line of them walked toward some place in the distance, a place he would never be able to go. He watched as someone else met with his family members, someone like him—a new soul. He saw them hugging, welcoming him into the fold. Envy tasted bitter on Patrick's tongue.

CHAPTER TEN

It was cold. Frigid. It was almost as if the Arcadians took the warmth with them when they left. Patrick stood looking at the place where his mother, great-great grandmother, and all of the other deceased relatives on his mother's side disappeared and felt a profound sadness, a sense of great loss. He had never known most of them—during his life he had only met an uncle and a handful of cousins: the result of a less than close-knit family—but, because of love, a sense of commitment, or both, they had chosen to meet him at the gate, to welcome him and show him the way. The sentiment touched him. The fact that he would never see his family again made him mourn for them and for himself. The uncertainty of what lay beyond frightened him more than he was willing to admit.

Joanne…

The place where Patrick stood was barren, oddly empty. A veil of white hung in the air, as much like fog or mist as it was different than them. He turned right and left, neither direction calling to him, neither route better than the other. He sighed, breathing in air that suddenly smelled sour. As it entered his nostrils and coursed down his nasal passages to his lungs, he realized something that he never expected to happen again, something that he never thought *could* happen again: He was breathing.

"Kind of shocks you when it starts back up again, don't it?"

Patrick looked up to find a man standing in front of him where none had stood before. He was an older guy, about 65 from the looks of him. He was naked, as all the others were, his body weathered and hunched from years of hard work in the sun. Blood soaked the side of his head, blending into the ridges of his skin like wax, streaking his face like war paint. His hair, wet with blood and matted, was flecked with tiny fragments of bone and tissue.

Patrick winced as he turned away.

The man smirked. "Hard to take, huh?" He shifted his weight. His southern drawl put Patrick at ease, like it would have when he was among the living. He managed to bring his eyes to the man's face.

"What the old gal forgot to tell you was that here you see what death really looks like."

Patrick felt like the wind had been knocked out of him. The thought of seeing people's wounds—gunshots, stabbings, the crushed bones of jumpers, the bloated faces of drowning victims—made him feel sick.

Patrick found himself taking panting breaths. He stopped breathing, holding in the last bit of air he'd sucked in, and was surprised to feel the burning in his lungs as they cried out for oxygen.

The man laughed, the frayed, ruined flesh on the side of his head jiggling as he moved. "Can't believe it, can you?"

"How can I breathe? Why?" Patrick managed.

"Because the rules of death are out the window. God, the Devil, they don't care about us. We don't exist to them. Our souls are unclaimed, so, instead of floating around like angels, our last image sticks and forms a body around us. We're skin and bones, like before. This way our soul has something to dwell in, even if our bodies don't."

Patrick raised his forearm to his face and saw the skin that covered it. It was his; he would have recognized his scattering of moles anywhere. Nostalgically he noted the bronze hue that sat on his skin and remembered his trip to the Caribbean a couple of weeks before he died. His embittered laughter sounded foreign to his ears, yet was more real than anything he had experienced since taking his last breath.

"Where is this?" Patrick asked, a mixture of confusion and fear boiling within him.

The man laughed again; this time the sound of his was voice coarse and brittle. "Where is this?" he hissed spitefully. "*This* is everywhere."

Patrick hesitated before offering, "The Realm?"

"Yes and no," the man replied. "The Realm is everything. Abaddon, Arcadia, and Atonement. But those places are like houses on a street. We are the street. We don't have the walls or force fields surrounding us like they do. Our region is vast and open. So, to answer your question, we are in the Great Nothingness."

Patrick let his mind work over what the old man told him. He couldn't shake the feeling that the whole thing was nothing more than an elaborate dream. But damn it, he knew better.

"I'm Bill Patterson," the man said, matter-of-factly. Rage built in Patrick fast, shooting up like a geyser before returning to the pit of his stomach.

"Are you the reason I'm here? Are you the reason my son will end up here?" He was ready for a fight. Patrick moved close, nose to nose with the old guy with the ruined face.

"No, no, son. Easy does it," Bill said, his hands raised in supplication. "I'm not kin to you. You'd want to take that up with them, not me. If you can."

Patrick remembered that Mark said the bastard was probably already in Abaddon and dropped his hands in frustration. The coward. Patrick hoped there would come a day when he would meet the man, the reason his whole line was damned, if only to snap his neck.

"Let's get moving. We shouldn't stay out in the open too long."

Patrick followed Bill, treasuring the feeling of his muscles contracting with every movement, but he stopped after only a couple of steps. "How do I know you're not a Hunter?" The concept was more real now that he had skin and bones.

Bill turned to Patrick and said, "You're smart to wonder. After all, I could be. You wouldn't have any way of knowing. Yet. But boy, once you've seen one of 'em, you'll never wonder if me or anyone else that looks human is a Hunter. They're like nothing you've ever seen before."

A breeze pushed Patrick's hair off his forehead. It felt incredible against his skin, like nothing he had ever felt before. His senses were renewed, heightened in his refurbished body. He had to fight the urge to close his eyes and relax into it.

"Come on," Bill said as he shook Patrick's arm. His touch was rough, jarring. Patrick snapped to attention. "They're coming. Let's go!"

Bill turned and ran into the void, the Great, colorless Nothingness, disappearing in the haze. Patrick followed behind him, running to keep up, running to escape the fear crawling up his spine.

CHAPTER ELEVEN

Bill ran with a younger man's dexterity through the void and into a forest with towering oaks and evergreens. As Patrick fought to keep pace with Bill, he realized that the muscles in his legs were burning. He could feel his feet pounding the solid ground, could feel his thighs pumping. He could almost hear his blood rushing through his veins. *How can this be?* he wondered as he felt cool sweat fall from his brow and land on his forehead. "Holy shit," he said, hardly realizing he had spoken aloud.

Bill's arms moved rhythmically, back and forth keeping time with his legs. He was frightened; Patrick could almost smell his fear in the air. He wanted to slow down and ask Bill what was so terrifying about the Hunters. How bad could they be? he rationalized. They were dead already after all, weren't they? But the irrational fear that permeated his body, his soul told him to keep going.

Patrick kept his legs moving, climbing rolling hills, jumping over logs, and sidestepping rocky patches along with Bill. It seemed to him that they had covered two miles, more than he had ever been able to run while he was alive.

The air in front of him was cool, but Patrick began to feel warmth where there hadn't been any before. It was coming from behind him, gaining on him.

The night crept in as they ran and darkness filled every crevice, every hole. The wind picked up; the susurrant rustling of the leaves sounded like the whispering of demons. Goosebumps raised on Patrick's skin like anthills along the forest floor. Bill was unaffected. It was as if he didn't hear the murmuring at all. He seemed to be in the zone, as though running was all he knew, his legs pinwheeling like a cartoon character. Even when Patrick called to him, mentioning the warmth behind him, he said nothing. His legs just kept pumping.

Patrick decided to look over his shoulder, to see the thing that chased them. He wanted to lay eyes on The Hunter. He felt his stomach drop before he did, his body reacting to the terror of having his tormentor revealed. He went with his gut and didn't look, too afraid to see what was back there. But it was too late. It had caught up to them at last. The Hunter filled Patrick's head with its existence, blocking out everything else that had been there before.

Patrick's legs almost stopped moving. He almost stood still in front of the thing, and would have were it not for the cold fear in the pit of his stomach. Patrick's mind almost couldn't wrap around what he was seeing. The thing's green skin was spotted with spiny appendages and covered by a gelatinous membrane. Pus-filled sacks floated on top of the skin, just beneath the viscous film. Its bilious green eyes stared out of jagged slits in the skin encased by a protective membrane. Tentacles writhed atop its hairless head in between four massive horns, leaning in Patrick's direction as though they could sense him. The Hunter stood on two legs and even hunched over, its formless girth was more massive than ten men. It had two arms with hands that resembled talons. The palms of its hands were affixed with suctions, like mouths, opening and closing as they reached for him.

Patrick couldn't hold in the scream that blared from his mouth. He wretched as though vomiting from the sight of the thing. Its skin glistened like that of a frog as Patrick's feet slapped at the ground awkwardly, desperately trying to go faster. It was amused.

Patrick turned away from the thing and ran with everything he had. He pushed himself, siding up to Bill and leading by a nose for the first time. Bill turned off the main road abruptly, reaching out to grab Patrick at the last second. They descended the hill on their heels, hitting the surface at an angle and kicking up dirt in clouds. Bill rolled to the right at the bottom of the hill. Patrick did the same. They hid behind a massive birch and a cluster of overgrown bushes, burrowing themselves in the fallen leaves. The Hunter didn't follow them down the hill. It stayed on top of it, standing to its full height as it surveyed the area. Patrick thought of a sports utility vehicle while looking at the creature, realizing that the thing would stand taller than one and be almost as wide.

"What the fuck is that thing?" Patrick whispered, his voice frantic.

"Shh. Its hearing is better than any animal you could think of."

Patrick looked back at the thing and saw that it was looking in their direction. It was looking right at him.

After what seemed like forever, the beast turned away and left. Its footsteps echoed through the forest like trees falling in the distance. He hadn't noticed the sound before.

"It knew we were here," Patrick said a long while after The Hunter left.

Bill nodded as he stood, brushing the leaves from his clothes. "It did. Sometimes it plays with us, especially with the new ones. It likes you scared. The kill is sweeter that way."

CHAPTER TWELVE

Patrick was lost in his thoughts on the walk to what would be his bedroom for the night. Bill led the way in silence, letting Patrick have time to himself.

Patrick's thoughts were jumbled, bouncing around in his head like a yoyo on a string. He was dead, yet he walked again, could smell again, could feel the air on his skin. There was an afterlife, though it was nothing like what he expected. At least not for him. The 'Heaven' that people talked about was Arcadia, a place he had only glimpsed, but that he would never be able to visit. The 'Hell' he had been taught to fear was real too, but he would never experience it either. He couldn't stop wondering what Hell must be like, if such a beast as the Hunters inhabited the Great Nothingness. He shuddered at the thought.

Patrick was in limbo.

He was nothing.

No one.

Unseen by God and the Devil.

He ceased to exist.

He wondered if rotting in the grave entombed in a gaudy box, eternally asleep, unaware, and oblivious—as dead as a doornail, as his son Doug had been fond of saying—was better than suffering in no man's land.

And it was all because of one person. One son of a bitch who botched it up for everyone else in his line. It gave him a headache to think of all the people in the Great Nothingness that would be related to him, all people who didn't deserve to be cast out of reach of Heaven and Hell. It was incredible when he stopped to think about it. Some bastard did something so terrible he blotted out his entire lineage. What could have been so massive, so important? Murder? Rape? There was Hell for those who savored blood, so what could it be? A chill crept up Patrick's spine as the sweat that dampened his skin cooled in the breeze. He wasn't so sure he wanted to know.

The truth of his situation resonated in him like the blaring of a loud horn: He was dead. He was cursed. He was one of The Hunted. His brand of cynicism crept in and made itself home in his thoughts, as comfortable in this new body as it had been in the old: He was fucked.

Chapter Thirteen

"You can set up right over there," Bill said, gesturing to the level patch of land near an outcropping of weeds and tall grass.

"We sleep outside?" Patrick asked incredulously, eying the spot on the ground that was to be his home in the afterlife. A memory, faint and fleeting, came back to him of a time when he and his father had gone camping behind the house. He was young, not more than six years old, and he didn't want to sleep outside. Not when his mother was inside where it was warm, where there was running water and hot chocolate, where there was television and the radio. "It'll be fun. You'll see," his father said. But it wasn't. It was as boring as he thought it would be. He hated it: the sound the bugs made when they rubbed their legs together, chirping in that awful high-pitched drone, how hard the ground was, even under his sleeping bag, the smell of the marshmallows they had burned mixing with the dank earth. He vowed to never do it again. And he didn't. He looked at the patch of land that seemed oddly like the place his father had picked to set up camp behind their house, and sighed.

"Yup, this is it. Beautiful, ain't it?" Bill was busy dusting off his ground covering to notice the look of distaste on Patrick's face.

"What about a house? Why do we have to live outside... like animals?" Patrick was beginning to wonder if everyone he'd met after death had lied to him and he was, in fact, in Hell.

Bill turned from his busy work and looked Patrick in the eye. He stared at him, through him, the corners of his mouth twitching. "I think you answered your own question, son."

Patrick looked away from the old man's face and let his eyes fall on his surroundings. The area was thick with trees, some living with lush foliage, some dead, nothing more than brittle branches. He listened. There weren't any bugs. He sniffed. There wasn't any discernible smell. He stamped the ground and found that it gave easily enough under the weight of his foot. It was softer than he remembered the ground being when he was alive.

If he squinted, if he looked really hard, he could see faint outlines of people, solid people, walking around the same woods, sharing the same space.

Patrick rubbed his eyes, more so to clear his vision of the living than out of need and noticed a structure in the distance. It had a steepled roof and three visible sides. There might have been a door, although shadowed and almost indistinguishable.

"What's that, way out there? That's a house, isn't it?" Patrick couldn't conceal the excitement in his voice.

Bill shook his head before saying, "You don't need to go worrying about that, Patrick. It's none of your concern."

"What? I'm not a fucking child, Bill. Don't tell me to ignore it." Patrick turned toward him, intensity making his cheeks hot.

"Who lives there?"

Bill went back to his patch of land and sat down silently. Patrick followed, sitting in front of him with anxious eyes.

"Well?" he urged.

"You'd only be asking for trouble," Bill said, worry thickening his voice.

"I won't tell anyone you told me about it. I'm new. I'll tell them I stumbled on it."

"I'm not worried about me. I'm worried about you."

"Don't worry about me. I can take care of myself," Patrick said, spitting the words out faster than he meant to. "Who lives there?"

Bill started the story he intended to tell Patrick later, after he had settled in. Bill had hoped that Patrick would have become preoccupied watching his granddaughter learning to walk, dancing at recitals. He figured he'd start the conversation about the Great Nothingness with Patrick when he grew to accept his lot and was content to see his family from a distance. Bill didn't expect to tell him so soon, on his first real night in The Realm. Telling Patrick meant he would move on, and Bill craved the companionship. But there was no way to keep it from him – Patrick was a man on a mission.

With a deep breath and a quick glance over his shoulder, Bill started.

Chapter Fourteen

Sebastian and Tara knelt in the bushes near where Bill and Patrick sat, straining to hear their conversation. Sebastian worked the bark of the tree with his knife absently, cutting into it easily with its makeshift double blade.

"He doesn't waste any time, does he?" Sebastian marveled.

"He's the fastest one yet." Tara homed in on Patrick's voice as he asked about the house.

"I hope he joins us," Sebastian adds. "He has more of a reason to than any of us did."

Tara's face, already pensive, clouded over, turning her delicate nose and high cheekbones into chiseled, stone features, hard and cold. Sebastian nodded imperceptibly before turning back to Bill and Patrick.

'Don't worry about me. I can take care of myself,' they overheard Patrick say.

"I hope so," Tara whispered.

CHAPTER FIFTEEN

Patrick awoke not realizing he had fallen asleep in the first place. The sun was rising, casting a muted golden ray in the distance. On the house. Bill's story sounded like a fairytale, one out of The Brothers Grim stable.

He laughed bitterly, loudly. His voice was louder than he meant it to be, but it didn't bother Bill. What a joke it had all been. Life. Patrick thought about how he had spent his days when he was alive. Spending too much time at work and not enough with his family. He was trying to get their retirement set up so they could have fun later on. How stupid it all was. His wife died before him, leaving him to suffer middle age by himself, just when life was supposed to get good. He had his son, sure, but Doug had his own life and Patrick understood that. He exercised for most of his adult life, but he still died. Just like everybody else.

And now, after he had lived a life that, in the end, had no meaning, after he had prayed to a god that didn't acknowledge his existence, he had to run.

Forever.

Patrick remembered being a kid and not wanting to go to church. His mother had been partial to one of those holy roller churches where members of the congregation called for Jesus and wailed with such fervor, a passerby might think pigs were being slaughtered inside if not for the worn, chipped sign out front. People just so happened to fall and land right where the preacher had lain a sheet just moments before. Those so filled with the Holy Spirit they couldn't stop themselves from thrashing about and flinging themselves around, had the presence of mind to flatten their skirts so they didn't show their privates in God's house. The men nodded their heads vigorously, chanting 'Hallelujah! Yes, Lord! Hallelujah!' and the woman pressed their eyes shut, put their hands in the air, and shouted, 'Thank you Lord! Thank you Jesussssssss!'— the word was so exaggerated that even in his adult life Patrick's inner voice hissed it like a snake. Those who weren't chanting, falling, spinning, or having what looked like an epileptic fit were somber, as though moved beyond words or actions. Including his mother. Patrick remembered the feeling of laughter welling in his chest, finding its way into throat and seeping into his mouth where it would be trapped there for as long as he could hold it, which wasn't very long at all. His mother would nudge him and frown, embarrassed, but Patrick couldn't help it. It all seemed so fake, so staged. He couldn't understand why no one else saw it but him.

That's how he felt now. Like he was the only one who got the joke, like he was awake and everyone else was asleep, like he was the man on the moon. And in the woods with his companion sleeping soundlessly—the sleep of the dead—that was easy to believe.

Patrick sat in silence looking out at the dawn that faded into day. He marveled at how time moved in this new existence. It was almost as though between blinks the sky transformed, the night's black sky turning to midnight blue within seconds. But never while he watched. It was like a little man ran out between the flutter of his eyelids to change the landscape, to color it with little paintbrushes and chalk.

The house was a ramshackle, windowless lean-to that you could find 20 miles past the Virginia border into West Virginia. Each slat seemed to know his name, seemed to pulse with life. The image ran together then pulled apart over and over, like fragments in a kaleidoscope, ever-moving, enticing his eyes to watch, to keep watching, to stare. Patrick saw a woman walk by the cloudy window that faced the forest where he hid. The sigh was fleeting but familiar. Joanne. It was her. He felt it in his bones.

"Early riser. That'll serve you well here."

Patrick jumped, startled, the shock evoking the familiar warmth in the pit of his stomach as his stomach leapt into his throat. Patrick hadn't heard the man get up, hadn't noticed the sound of rustling the leaves must have made. That scared him.

"How can you be so calm?" Patrick spat, the anger with him rising to a boil faster than he expected it to. He needed to get it out somehow and lashing out at Bill seemed as good a way as any. "You act like living here and hiding like animals is ok. Well, it's not ok, Bill. It's bullshit!"

"You think I don't get angry? You think I don't hate the god who turned his back on me and the devil who didn't care enough to scrape me off the bottom of his shoe? Of course, I do, but hating them doesn't help you in The Realm. Hate'll only slow you down."

Patrick shook his head, the sensibility of what Bill said calming him a bit. "I don't deserve this."

"Neither do I, my friend. My daddy always said that dead is dead. He didn't go in for all that religion stuff, and neither did I. I wish he had been right."

Bill grew quiet as he and Patrick stared out at the house looming before them. Through the tangle of branches, they could see the worn siding and rusted girders. The sight of shelter, rickety or not, filled Patrick with jealousy.

"Mileeha sees you. You don't think he can, not from behind those walls, but believe me, he does."

Bill stared at the house with eyes filled with reverent fear rimming the perimeter of his dark brown irises. The early morning darkness couldn't conceal his fear.

"Mileeha?" Patrick asked as he turned back to look at the house. Its broad side was illuminated by the rays of the morning sun.

"He's probably the biggest Hunter of them all. Second in command under Mal. That Hunter that chased us yesterday was as harmless as a baby compared to him."

Patrick turned to look at Bill whose gaze at the house never wavered. "Why the hell do you camp so close to the worst Hunter in The Realm?" Patrick's voice was louder than he intended it to be.

"They don't want me. I'm old. Rotten. Too easy to catch. My flesh isn't sweet and tender like yours is." The hair on the nape of Patrick's neck stood on end. For a moment Bill no longer looked like the weathered old man who was nice enough to help him, to save him from the Hunter on the road, to show him the ropes. For a fleeting second, his face resembled a Hunter of another kind, the smell of blood flaring his nostrils and coloring his eyes. Patrick recoiled, unable to shake the thought.

"I've been here for a long time, boy, longer than you think. If they wanted to kill me, they would have done it years ago. The musket that killed me was leveled to my head at Raisin River in 1813. They've had time enough to do something with me if they intended to."

"So why haven't they?" Patrick asked hesitantly.

"Because they needed someone to show the newcomers the ropes. They figured out that we taste better when we're scared, and only fear of what was to come would keep us on edge all the time. Knowing the thing that comes for you can think and plan, is enough to keep us awake at night. And that's just how they like it.

"So, you're setting me up?" Patrick didn't know whether to run or beat the old man senseless.

"No. I'm trying to arm you. I'm giving you information that could save your life. A lot of times what I tell people goes ignored. Everybody thinks they know best. But without me you would have run right up to the house and knocked on the door. A Hunter would have eaten your legs before you even knew he was there."

Patrick looked at the old man and believed him. There was no malice in his eyes; there was no joy in telling the story. All Patrick saw was a man who had accepted his lot and tried to help others do the same.

"But the Hunter on the road chased you too."

Bill sloughed off the memory with a wave, "A Parasic. Brainless animals that only know how to chase. They're like the Hunter's bloodhounds. Parasics will be the least of your worries. But if they catch you, they'll kill you just the same."

Bill stared back at the house and lowered his voice instinctively. "But Mileeha wouldn't be happy about that. He would want to make sure you were tortured first. He has a pit somewhere in the Great Nothingness. I-" Bill stuttered and shot a quick glance at Patrick before looking away. "I've heard terrible stories of games and human flesh being served as an entrée to Mal."

Patrick couldn't hide the revulsion he felt. He turned back to the house. The sun had risen around them and the sky was blue and clear.

Bill grabbed Patrick's shoulder roughly and said, "You can't stay here, Patrick. You have to move on."

"What?" Patrick felt like his world was turning upside down. Without realizing it, he had gotten used to the old man, despite his concerns, despite his fear.

"It's not safe for you here, not anymore, if it ever was." Bill's voice was grave.

"What are you talking about? I just got here."

"But you know too much. About the Hunters, about Mileeha. You know more than any prey has ever known after their first night in The Realm... more than you should."

A sound, like a door slamming, came from the house. Bill crouched lower in the thick, pulling Patrick with him and watched. Nothing.

"You can't be here anymore. This place is for new prey to learn about the world around them, to prepare them for eternity. You're safe here when you're learning. They know you're here; they can smell you, but the scent isn't as strong, isn't as appetizing as it is when you know enough to be afraid. Scared, down in your bones. And you do now. You know everything I had to teach you. You know what and who to be afraid of. You know why you're running, and you know it's not only about the blood, but it's about the game. The hunt. And they know you know."

"But I don't know anything! Not enough to be on my own." Patrick felt like a child admitting it, but it was true.

"Yes, you do. And you'll have to prove it soon enough." Bill shook his head and turned away from Patrick. His tentative step was echoed by the cracking of a twig underfoot. "I told you to let me wait and tell you in my own time, but you pressed me."

Patrick's stomach felt queasy. He was terrified. As the old man crawled away, he called to him. "Bill! I'm not ready to be alone. Not yet. I-," he hesitated, pride taking over for an instant before winking out, "I don't know where to go."

Bill turned back to look at Patrick, as small as a boy lost in the woods. "You'll figure it out soon enough," he said with a gentle voice and kind eyes. "You'd better."

Bill turned away and moved on, crawling at a snail's pace, trying not to call attention to where Patrick sat. He knew they were watching, knew they would watch until sundown, and then they'd send a Parasic to track him, scare him a little, tease him. They craved the smell of his fear, musky and pungent. It tantalized their nostrils like the smell of a steak on the barbeque.

CHAPTER SIXTEEN

Tara watched Patrick long after Sebastian went back to camp. She was used to being in the woods alone; even when she was alive, she had an affinity for it. It was calming somehow, the rustling of leaves, the whisper of tree limbs in the wind. She would lose herself in the woods near her uncle's house, spending the entire day exploring. It was like her second home.

She smelled it before she heard its heavy footfalls. A Hunter. The first time she saw one of them she ran for her life. But since then she and her friends – they called themselves the Watchers– had figured out the way to kill them. Sometimes they ate the Hunters but most times they just killed them because they could. To the watchers, the Hunters were prey.

With her spear gripped tightly in her hand, Tara turned toward the sound and followed it.

**

Sebastian, Kincaid, and Aadi were still asleep when Tara came back to the camp, the smell of death on her skin. Qiao and Lydjauk watched the sunrise from the hill that concealed their camp as they did every morning, laying flat on their backs, watching the color of night change to day as the sun rose behind them.

"It's beautiful," Lydjauk said, its uppermost eye staring into the sun's brilliant light while the eyes that were nested in its forehead watched the sky change color. "I never get used to seeing it."

"What does it look like?" Qiao asked excitedly.

"Why not see for yourself?"

"I can't look at it, I've told you that."

"Can't you?" Lydjauk allowed one eye to stare at Qiao while the other two watched the exit of night and the entrance of day. "You've never tried before."

"Humans can't look directly into the sun. It'll burn our retinas. We'll go blind."

"But you're not human any more than you're Chinese or than I'm Black, are you Qiao?" Tara asked as she bounded over the hill. Her shadow stretched long and angular behind her. "You're nothing. Dead and gone. Dead as a doorknob. Wood for the furnace-"

"Jesus," Qiao exclaimed and frowned at Tara, the smirk on her face stirring rage within him. He got up and walked away from the spot where he and Lydjauk watched the sunrise everyday and skulked into the woods surrounding their camp.

"Don't get lost. I have something tell you," Tara called after him. Qiao didn't respond but perched in the crook of a tree just the same.

"Why do you tease him, Tara? You know he needs time to adjust." The fleshy skin around Lydjauk's face, like hair matted with blood, pulled into itself, as though retreating from Tara. All three of its eyes were trained on her, their lids, like steepled hoods, hanging low over its colorless, pupil-less eyes. It was as close to a frown as the Venian could get.

"For the same reasons you do, Lydjauk, Tara said, her almost black eyes dancing.

The Venian's mouth, nothing more than a gaping hole of blackness with no discernible teeth or tongue among the writhing mass of gel-covered flesh, pursed in what would have been a coy fashion had it been struck by a beautiful woman before turning all three of its eyes to the sun.

Tara shook Sebastian, Kincaid, and Aadi hard to wake them up. She waited until their protests died down before she spoke.

"He's on the move," she announced, her voice a mixture of glee and surprise.

"Already?" Aadi asked, yawning as he did.

"He just got here. What, did the old man get sick of him already?" Kincaid chimed in.

"Time for a sacrifice to the Hunters in exchange for good favor, probably," Lydjauk added.

"Good favor," Kincaid sneered, "It's called covering his ass."

Sebastian's eyes danced but he said nothing.

Tara shook her head. "The old man prepared him the same way he prepared us."

"But it took us weeks to understand The Realm!" Qiao said, strolling toward them.

"Some of us still don't get it," Kincaid said, staring at Qiao all the while.

"He took all of the instruction in one night," Tara fought not let the smile she felt burning her cheeks show on her face.

"One night?" Lydjauk said, standing up from the hill and stretching to his full, nearly 8ft height before making his way over to the rest of the group. "He's as good as dead."

"I don't know about that," Sebastian said, running a hand through his hair.

"How could he survive? He barely knows the difference between The Realm and the Great Nothingness!" Aadi's sounded genuinely concerned.

"He'll survive the same way we did," Sebastian said calmly. "He'll find us, and when he does, we'll be there for him."

CHAPTER SEVENTEEN

Patrick's first night alone in the place that was to be his home for eternity was met with trepidation and fear. He hoped it would go away, would dissipate as the fog over his vision now seemed to when he looked out at the city streets and laid eyes on the living. But he knew it wouldn't. Fear was to become a part of him. He would wear like a coat, like the very skin that tensed beneath his touch.

Bill hadn't answered the questions Patrick had hurled at him in the waking morning, at least not enough to satisfy him. He asked why he had to leave and Bill told him he must go before they come for him. He asked why they wanted him so badly and Bill told him that he was prey, nothing more and nothing less. He asked what he was supposed to do, and Bill told him to run.

So, he did.

Patrick ran through the Great Nothingness, putting distance between himself and the house. He had no idea where he was or where he was supposed to go but still he ran, like the devil himself was on his heels.

Patrick found level ground and made camp, gathered stones to form a pit for a fire, piled leaves and twigs on top of each other to burn before he realized he had nothing to cook. The weight of reality fell on shoulders like a rock that had been dropped from high above him. He would starve if he couldn't find food. Would starve, but he wouldn't die. The pains in his stomach assured him that the lack of nourishment would be felt, that his body would be wracked with pain and weak. Still, he wouldn't die. He would he be damned to suffer in pain for eternity? What differentiated Hell from The Great Nothingness if that was to be his fate?

Existence.

His stomach churned as he looked around in search of something to eat. There were no animals. Patrick smirked, remembering his Bible Study teacher, an ancient nun from the old country with an accent so thick he couldn't understand a word she said half the time, telling him that his dog wouldn't be in Heaven with him because dogs didn't go to Heaven. Because animals don't have souls. *Where are you now, Sister?* Patrick thought ruefully. Only birds of prey that seemed on the lookout for the Hunters soared in the sky, stretching their incredible wings to blot out the sun.

And Parasics.

Bill told him not to worry about the things he normally would have when he was alive. He said they didn't exist in The Realm, not in the way that they had before. So far, he was right.

The night air was cold; the chill of the wind covered him like second skin, yet, Patrick couldn't see his breath. Even though he could feel himself inhaling and exhaling, drawing the air into his lungs he couldn't see it when he exhaled in the cold night. His skin raised goosebumps on his flesh, but he did not shiver.

CHAPTER EIGHTEEN

Heavy steps awoke Patrick after what seemed like a minute's worth of sleep, thumping, thundering, vibrating the earth with ever footfall. Leaves crunched underfoot; trees splintered. He thought he was dreaming, even though his senses snapped him alert the moment the first tremor coursed through him. The day was in full bloom; the sun had already risen overhead, and humidity thickened the air.

A Parasic.

Patrick bolted upright. He had to run. Fast.

The terrain was as unfamiliar to him in daylight as it was in the dark of night. Images from the world he used to live in shone through the haze, confusing him. A battered garbage can lay on its side on the leaf-covered plain, a brick wall; one-sided and seeming to reach up from the ground from nothing, towards nothing, connected to nothing, stood discarded on the grass, separating the knoll from the stream that gurgled behind it. Patrick stumbled onward, through the wall, half wondering if he was going to smack into it. But he passed through it, and that reality almost drove Patrick to his knees.

He could feel the Parasic's hot breath on his neck.

Patrick bounded over fallen trees like an Olympic hurdler, making moves he had never even attempted while living. But still the thing drew closer and closer to him, toying with him.

Patrick ran faster than he ever had. The thought of the Parasic's fangs dripping with saliva in anticipation of piercing his flesh terrified him. Would it hurt? Would he bleed like he would have when he was alive? Of course, he would. He was sure of it.

With every step he took, Patrick either crunched leaves underfoot or broke twigs. Even when he ran on the open ground, his footfalls seemed to vibrate through the soil and make an audible *thump*. He was sweating, almost crying, his fear boiling over. Bill told him what the Parasics were. He told him what would happen if they or any of the Hunters caught him. He didn't want to be one of those grotesque, half man, half wildebeest things mindlessly tracking people down, mauling them and offering up their carcasses as more converts for the cause.

Patrick ran blindly, unaware of where the path led, not knowing if he would come upon a camp of Parasics waking in the morning light. Or worse. When a hand reached out from the underbrush and grabbed his leg, causing him to trip and fall head over heels onto the rock-hewn path, he screamed outloud.

Wide eyes almost as frightened as his stared out at him from a dirt streaked face. The man behind the grime poked his lips out and put his fingers to them with such fervor, he pressed the chapped skin flat. Patrick nodded and scurried into the embankment where the man sat, too scared to worry about whether he had just stepped into a trap. Pressing themselves close to the ground where dirt and leaves waited to stick to their sweaty bodies, they listened for the Parasic. Patrick was sure it had been right behind him.

They waited for what seemed like an hour but the Parasic never hefted its bulk onto the patch of road where they hid.

"Our fear is like bloody perfume to them."

The British lilt his voice took made the comment incredibly funny to Patrick, and he laughed open-mouthed and unabashed. The man, surprised by Patrick's laughter, pressed himself closer to the embankment and spat, "Shut your trap! These things hear from miles on."

Patrick tried to control himself, but he couldn't seem to get a grip on the tickle in the back of his throat. It was then, when the laughter brought tears to his eyes, he realized that he would either laugh or cry.

The man looked around, his brow furrowing on top of his lined forehead. Satisfied that nothing was coming, he settled into a groove he had worn in the sand. He had been hiding in that embankment since he got The Great Nothingness. How long ago was that? He wasn't exactly sure. But he knew he'd been there longer than Patrick. He remembered what new felt like.

"What's your name?" the man asked, sticking a twig in his mouth and rolling it to nestle between his back teeth and his cheek. "Or can't you say as yet for the fit your pitching?"

The man looked away, casually glancing up the road, watching the morning unfold in the land of the living. That spot in The Great Nothingness was an apartment complex on Earth in the real world. A young mother wrestled with a garbage bag while holding her baby in her other arm. The shiner she sported made him shut his eyes in disgust.

"Patrick. My name's Patrick."

The man turned toward him and nodded. He extended his hand absently. "The name's Dominic."

Patrick shook his hand as he recovered from the last shuddering laugh. "Thank you for pulling me off the road," he said.

"Don't mention it. Rather not see a bloke get torn to bits before my eyes is all." Dominic turned to look at the woman, too skinny and haggard in a way that meant she'd lived a hard life, as she sighed, jiggled the plump baby on her bony hip.

Patrick looked past Dominic, trying to see what he saw. "What are you looking at?"

Dominic looked at Patrick sternly at first, then lightened his stare. "It's nothing." He shifted the twig in his mouth. "She's my sister. This is her flat," he replied to Patrick's silence.

"You watch her?" Patrick asked, stepping closer as he peered through the haze, trying to make the woman's shape out. For him the haze was still thick, though not as much as before. He could see shadows of another world, like ghosts lingering in the doorway of a darkened room, but he couldn't make out features. He wondered if Joanne could see Doug.

"Yes, though I know she would hate the intrusion if she knew," Dominic said, his voice thick. "Or would she? I wonder sometimes about that." Patrick looked after the woman, straining to see her. For a moment he thought he saw the doorframe of the apartment, but he wasn't sure. "So, it doesn't get any better? You don't get over it."

"What? Living? I suppose that depends upon your state of mind when you left. For me the leaving was easy. But letting her go, that I'll never get used to."

Patrick cast a quick glance at Dominic, intrigued. He scanned him, searching for the wound that killed him, and found it high on his hip. The cut was deep and wide; Patrick could see the inflamed skin inside the gash, bright red surrounded by greenish exposed tissue. Though he wanted to question, Patrick didn't, turning away instead. He was suddenly ashamed. He too held his own battle scars.

When Patrick laid his eyes on the spot where he had looked before, he saw a woman's figure walking up trash littered steps and into a rundown apartment building.

Patrick was walking before he knew it, following her. He passed cars the way he would have if he was alive, walking between them, being careful not to hit the review mirror.

"So, careful, yeah? Walk steady through and see." Dominic's voice sounded as though it was coming to him through a funnel. He turned toward him slowly, as though drugged. "What are you doing, man? You're dead! You can go straight through and you won't even rattle the bumper."

Patrick looked at the car in front of him, a late model sedan. Suddenly he wanted to be in the car, wanted to feel the leather seats beneath him, wanted to wrap his hands around the steering wheel. If only he could hit the gas and drive.

Patrick looked back at Dominic, whose grinning face would have been comical under different circumstances, before taking a step toward the car. Then through the car. The smell of leather—he always loved the smell of a new car—was tantalizing. He almost didn't want to leave the cabin.

"I've got a bloody virgin on my hands!" Dominic said, his voice having replaced the pain it carried with glee. "Well, come on then, let's see what the ole girl is up to, after all." Dominic clapped a hand on Patrick's back—he was still amazed that he could not only hear the slap of skin against skin, but he could feel it—and led him to the stairs.

Dominic's sister lived in a first floor apartment. The door was dirty. Painted with a glossy, thick taupe coat that had dried in solid, runny globs, the door seemed to have a light film of oily grime covering it. Patrick wanted to touch it, wanted the feel it beneath his hand, wanted to rub his fingers together and feel them slide against each other, slicked with filth. The idea both repulsed and enticed him. He almost reached out to it when Dominic spoke,

"This is it. She and my niece live here with… him." Dominic's face had grown angry.

"Him?"

"The wanker that carved me." His hand lingered protectively near his wound. "That bastard Kenneth."

Patrick nodded, not knowing what to say.

Dominic shook his head and continued, "She went arse over tit for him the year before it happened. I knew him from the pub; even the barmaid had a go! So, she wanted to shag him, didn't matter to me. Her business was her own. But when she started to get serious with him, I stepped in. He used to feel up the slappers at the pub, patting their arses and such. They said he put his hands on a couple of his dates too. I told Sheila—my sister's name is Sheila—he was a bleeding berk and to watch herself, but she told me to mind my own business. She could be such a clot sometimes, always taking up with crooked chaps, so I kept watch. Something about this one worried me.

"When Sheila told me she was up the duff I was pissed off. She-"

"What?" Patrick asked. He had been enjoying Dominic's dialect and his gruff demeanor. It reminded him of a college friend from "Blighty" as he called it. They had made plans for Patrick to visit his home in England throughout their years at the University, but he never made it there. The extent of his British slang had been reached and he was lost. "Up the duff?"

"Pregnant, man," Dominic said, cracking a smile that lit up his face. "A bun in the oven." Patrick nodded as Dominic continued. "She told me he popped a hole in his johnny—rubber?" He raised his eyebrows in question to Patrick. Patrick nodded again. "It was on purpose! I couldn't believe it. I mean, I love my niece, but bloody hell!"

Patrick looked back at the door. It was vivid, the cracks in the paint, the dull, worn knocker, and chipped keyhole. The whole thing blew his mind. He was looking at a door in a country he had never seen, and he got there by simply running down the road. He would have chuckled at the irony if Dominic's voice hadn't sounded so urgent.

"She stayed with the bastard even after what he did, God bless her," Dominic continued, his eyes trained on the clouded peephole.

Patrick felt the urge to lean closer to it and look through, maybe catch a glimpse of the woman again, but he dared not. "And she's still with him now.

The harsh edge to Dominic's voice gave way to a softness that Patrick wasn't ready to hear. It took everything he had not to turn and look at Dominic with sympathy in his eyes. With pity.

"When she was eight months on, he roughed her up a bit. She told me about it, and I took him out back of the bar to settle it man to man. That's when he did it." Dominic's hand covered the wound from view. His fingers pulled at either side, as though he wanted to hold the gash together.

"I never saw it coming. The coward got me with a dirty blade, as cold as a witch's tit. And then, I ended up here."

Patrick didn't know what to say. He wanted to ask how he found her, how he knew where to look in The Realm to see his sister. His lips parted and worked, trying to form the words, but nothing came out.

"So, I watch her," Dominic continued, oblivious to Patrick's tongue-tied confusion. "I come to her every morning and watch her get up and prepare the baby. I watch her as she kills herself with drugs and when she cries at the table in the nook. I watch as that bastard shags her like he like he doesn't have a care in the world. Sheila doesn't know he's the one he sent me to meet my maker. And nobody saw it happen. So, he's free and clear and I'm here running for my bloody life from goddamned monsters." Dominic took a deep breath and turned to face Patrick. His face lightened, like a weight had been lifted from his shoulders. With more levity in his voice than he had used since beginning his story, Dominic said, "But then so are you, old boy. We're in this together then." He clapped Patrick on the back before looking at the door again. "Let's go in, yeah? It's about time for my daily rounds."

Dominic took a step toward the door and walked through, disappearing before Patrick's eyes.

Patrick stood alone in the hallway of Sheila's building breathing heavily. He was afraid. Even though he had walked through a car outside, he was scared that somehow the magic would wear off and he would clonk his head on the door. *Human thoughts*, he admonished. *Alive thoughts.*

Patrick steeled himself, taking deep breaths that filled his lungs. His first step was small, infantile, like a child's first attempt at walking. His next took him through the door.

The room was dark. Though the day was bright, Sheila's apartment was on the backside of the building where an abandoned mill stood to block the light. And the view. The taupe paint on her walls was the same as the paint on her door and had dried in the same manner, as though one coat was too heavy to stick to the plaster and had dried on its way to the floor. No paintings or pictures hung on the walls. No mirrors reflected the sparse fittings to tired eyes.

Sheila's furniture was threadbare. The rugs that lay on the chipped linoleum were raggedy and thin. The smell of marijuana hung in the air.

Sheila's baby bounded into the room on shaky legs, running from a bedroom at the end of a dark hallway to the kitchen. Her chatter was like music to Patrick's ears. It made him think about the baby that Chris carried, gave him visions of his son Doug as a father. He didn't feel the tears that formed in his eyes.

Patrick walked ahead on legs that moved of their own volition, passing by where Dominic stood in the in the dinning room to stand in the doorway of the kitchen. He wanted to see the baby, wanted to take in as much of her as he could.

"My niece Christina," Dominic offered as he sided up with Patrick. "A beauty, yeah? Looks just like our mum."

Patrick nodded, the smile on his face genuine. "She's a beautiful girl."

"I never got to hold her." Dominic stared at his hands as he spoke. Patrick's expression crumbled as he listened to Dominic talk about his niece. He too would never hold his grandchild, would never kiss its little feet, its little hands. The child would never know him or Joanne. They would only know the pictures. The tears in his eyes spilled over onto his cheeks and he didn't raise a hand to wipe them away.

"I was so excited about her coming, but I never got to hold her," Dominic continued, fighting tears of his own. "Sheila almost lost her when she found out about me. I had to go to Mileeha and beg him to ask Mal to save her."

Hearing Mileeha's name spoken brought Patrick out of his despair and back into the world where he stood. His eyes searched Dominic's for lies, for trickery, for betrayal. "You spoke with Mileeha?" He couldn't hide the skepticism that laced his voice.

"I had to," Dominic said. If he detected Patrick's disbelief, he didn't show it. "I begged for my niece's life."

"And he did it for you? He spared her just because you asked him to?" Patrick eyed the door, gauging the distance in case he had to escape. He decided suddenly, with the speed, the overwhelming *being* of light filling a room once the switch on the wall has been flicked, that Dominic was lying. Either that or he was crazy. Either option made him dangerous.

"A life for a life he said, so I agreed," Dominic continued, suddenly weary.

Patrick had taken a step away without realizing it. "What does that mean?"

"It means that when he's ready—when he's hungry—he'll come for me and I won't fight it."

"You'll sacrifice yourself if there's no one else around to satisfy him?"

"There's always another." Dominic's voice was hard.

Patrick looked back at Christina playing with a string that dangled from Sheila's ill-fitting top, as Dominic did. It was a long time before either of them spoke again.

"Will she live a long life?" Patrick asked for want of something to say.

"If he is willing. That Mal could intervene at all means he has already claimed her as his own. If she does, it will only be to die a horrible death at some bastard's hand and be damned to run in The Great Nothingness. Just like me."

Patrick detected something in Dominic's voice that struck him as uncharacteristic, out of place. "You don't think you had anything to do with it, do you? All that stuff's predetermined. Fate and all that."

"Didn't I?" Dominic asked, looking Patrick squarely in the face. "What if that child's destiny was to die in her mother's womb and live life in Arcadia with the rest of our family? Or maybe some mother was waiting on her soul to come to them and be born to a happy life. Instead, I opened my mouth and damned that child to The Great Nothingness."

"You did it because you love her."

"You call that love?" Dominic's breath was hot. "I sent that girl to be born into a house where he father beats her mother and her mother is in a drug-induced fog all day. I sent her to a life where she crawls on filthy floors and her stomach cramps for the next meal. Then, when she dies painfully, I made her prey. Like me. All because I love her." Dominic looked back at the baby, grinning as she looked at the place where they stood, almost as if she could see them.

"So much for love, yeah?"

Christina turned back to Sheila and thumped her head on her chest. Dominic lowered his voice conspiratorially. He brought his lips close to Patrick's ear. "But if it was a trick, that changes things. I'll break the bastard in two before if I was duped into thinking Christina was dying when she wasn't.

Dominic cast one last glance at Sheila and Christina in the kitchen nook before walking toward the door. "Might as well get along then," he said with his back to Patrick, "I expect we have a lot of ground to cover."

CHAPTER NINETEEN

Patrick's urge to run dissipated as quickly as it had come. He felt comfortable with Dominic. At 5'7", he was shorter than Patrick by head and shoulders, yet he talked like a man over 7'0 tall, and from the stories he told, he had the mettle to prove it. He told Patrick about his many barroom fights and his trysts with women, all the while his wound glowed purplish red in the waning light. Patrick couldn't relate: he had been married to Joanne for thirty-five years before she died and hadn't done a whole lot of dating before or after. But he listened and nodded at the appropriate times, happy just to hear another person's voice.

Dominic told Patrick about his transition from life to death in vivid detail. Patrick felt goosebumps rise on his skin as Dominic spoke, his story so closely mirroring Patrick experience that it made him shiver.

Patrick was hyper-aware of the day passing, but he couldn't figure out just how fast it was going. Day turned to night, and night to day in a fraction of the time it took when he was alive. A day in the Great Nothingness could be two weeks, one month to the living. The idea made him sad. Part of his told him that Doug had forgotten about him. It said Doug's pain was over - hat he had moved on. He imagined Doug and Chris raising their new baby over their heads. He could almost see the line of spit that would extend from his grandson's (the baby was a boy, he was certain) lips to his son's smiling, upturned face. He should be happy about that, he knew, but he wasn't. The old hens his mother used to go around with used to nod their heads in old knowing unison when a baby was born on the cusp of a death. *God's will*, they'd repeat as they rocked. *One life for another.*

Of all the other things plaguing Patrick's mind - the Hunters, Mileeha, the fear that enveloped him, the thought, this feeling of being forgotten took precedence.

"Tell the truth, when you got here and figured out you were starkers, what did you do?"

Patrick turned to Dominic as though in a daze. He hadn't been listening to what Dominic was saying, wasn't aware the he was talking at all until then.

"I remember what I did," Dominic continued, oblivious. "I looked down to see if I had a stiffy." His voice trembled beneath his jovial tone.

"I want to see my family," Patrick blurted out. The words came as though a dam had broken and they were tumbling freely over his tongue and lips like fresh water.

"I want to see my family," Patrick repeated, an edge creeping into his voice that hadn't been there before. "How do we get to them?"

Dominic regarded Patrick for a moment in silence. He looked at the man, at how soft and manicured he was, at how his skin had never been ripped or bruised, scarred or scabbed. Everything about Patrick would have repulsed Dominic when he was alive. He imagined Patrick behind a desk rattling the keys laptop and calling it work, instead of getting his hands dirty. Everything about him was perfect: his hair his nails, even his waist — Patrick was in good shape, Dominic conceded. Everything fit. Except the bullet hole that opened his chest. But there, in The Realm, Dominic was happy to have found someone who hadn't been driven crazy by the Hunters yet, or who wasn't sent to kill him. At least, he didn't think Patrick was. He needed the company, needed to talk and share, to listen and laugh. He didn't know when his number would be up, but he knew it wouldn't be long. He wanted to spend the time he had left with someone.

But he would watch Patrick, all the same.

Dominic kicked Patrick's comment around a moment longer, enjoying the feeling of making him wait. After another quick glance at Patrick's wound, purpled to violet in the dimming light, Dominic nodded and said, "Of course you do, don't you?"

"I have to," Patrick said, not noticing Dominic measuring him up. He was too busy hoping his secrets were hidden from view. "Do you know how to get back to the United States?"

Dominic's laugh was rich. "The U.S., England, bloody China and Africa for all we know. Do you remember swimming the Atlantic before you bumped into me?"

Patrick's face showed confusion.

"Mate, all you did was take a couple steps before you ran into me. I bet you didn't travel more than 2 kilometers from where you joined the road." He clapped Patrick on the back and finally, Patrick's mood eased.

"How is this possible?" Patrick asked no one in particular as they walked back the way he had come. Patrick imagined that they were walking on the water, covering the Atlantic between the US and Europe in three or four strides. "How can we cross space and time the way we do? Where else can we go? To other planets?"

Dominic listened as Patrick's questions came in a deluge, much like his desire to see his family had. He was quiet not because he wanted Patrick to get what he felt off his chest, but because he didn't have any answers to give.

Dominic got lost in the world beyond them, the one where people went about their evening as they always would, oblivious of Patrick and Dominic standing right next to them. But not everyone was blind to them. Some did see them, like the little girl waiting with her father in a restaurant. People like her seemed to study them. Could they see his nakedness? Did they see the grotesque slash in his side? Dominic had his own set of question that had gone unanswered.

"Does any of this make sense to you?" Patrick asked urgently.

Dominic's mouth was dry. The little girl's stare hadn't wavered a bit.

"It makes as much sense as two dead man talking does, mate," Dominic offered, falling back on the humor that carried him through most of his tough times. He wondered what Patrick's failsafe was.

The deep, guttural grunt of a Hunter sounded in the distance. Chills ran down Patrick's spine.

"We better get moving," Patrick said. By the time the words made their way out of his mouth, they had already started to pick up their pace, crouching below the line of the view.

They followed Patrick's steps as he stumbled through the woods that morning, running from a Hunter.

Patrick was surprised he remembered the way he came, but he did. The land was nondescript but, in a way, that made it easier to navigate. With everything looking the same, he let his gut take over. And his gut had never failed him.

A sharp pain shot into Patrick's head as his gut reminded him of the time he hadn't listened. The time that cost him his life.

CHAPTER TWENTY

Lydjauk watched as Patrick and Dominic moved along the road. It too heard the growling of a nearby Hunter, but wasn't worried- its sense of smell was very sharp in The Realm, more so than it had been when it was alive.

Dominic and Patrick ran. To the two of them, the Parasic was too close to ignore. They were desperate to put distance between them. Lydjauk lurked in the woods, camouflaged among the trees, watching as they fled.

CHAPTER TWENTY-ONE

When they came to the clearing where Patrick had emerged from the woods and joined the road, Patrick veered off and took a step towards the tangle of trees.

"No, we'll stay on the road and look from here," Dominic said as he stopped. He looked into the distance, squinting

"Here?" Patrick asked. "Why should we stop here?"

Dominic chuckled but kept looking off at something Patrick couldn't quite make out. "Don't worry. I don't reckon we'll come across a bobby to send us back."

Patrick walked toward Dominic, even though he didn't quite get his meaning. He was intrigued now. He wanted to know what was so important to see.

Patrick looked past the haze and saw a busy suburban center with shops and a movie theater. A sweet shop offered a special on chocolate croissants and coffee and a bookstore promoted the author who would sign books at that location later that night. A movie theater listed the movies in its eight theaters and people pooled in front of it, buying tickets. It was a place Patrick knew.

It was where Doug lived.

"How did you know we were here? How could you possibly know that?" Patrick looked at Dominic with disbelieve. And there was something else that lurked within his dark eyes. Fear.

Dominic laughed, "I'm psychic, mate. A bloody card reader." His smile was met with an incredulous stare. Patrick looked as if he might jump out of his skin. He could see Patrick's distrust in his face and, though he could understand why, it still made him angry. He wanted to tell Patrick to piss off, to find his own way through The Realm, and to forget he ever met him, but something made him hold his tongue. "You look like you've seen a ghost," he said instead, his voice sounding a bit off, unable to disguise his mounting anger.

"How would you know? We're five miles away from where my son lives right now. Five miles! In fact, they could be here right now, shopping. That's too much of a coincidence, don't you think?" Patrick stared at Dominic, sizing him up. He didn't know what his new body could do. It felt like his old one, but if it wasn't, he would be at a disadvantage if it came down to a fight. If Dominic was a Hunter, he was dead.

Dominic took a deep breath before speaking. He reminded himself that Patrick was new and that he was still trying to understand what happened to him. He decided to cut the man some slack. Besides, he needed the company more than he cared to admit.

"When we set off on our own, our bodies bring us back the things we miss most. It's like a magnet, mate. It's sadistic. We never start out exactly where we need to be, but all that does is make us keep searching, day in and day out. When we finally look up, we're standing face to face with our sisters," Dominic paused, gauging Patrick, "or our sons."

Patrick looked back at the town center, at the throngs of people going in and out of stores and standing in front of the movie theater. They were oblivious to his staring eyes. They didn't see his nudity, his wound, gaping and discolored. They didn't see *him*. They just went about their routine, looking into shops he would never step foot in again and eating meals he would never enjoy. Patrick envied them so much that a pain surged in his chest. His bullet hole pulsed, the flesh trembling like a woman on the brink of orgasm. The feeling sickened him.

Dominic took a step toward Patrick while he gazed longingly at the world beyond his reach. He could read the emotion on Patrick's face, could see what being there did to him. Dominic felt genuinely sorry for him. He knew what it was like to see the world go on without you. "You can stop worrying about me," Dominic said. "I've been alone too long to put effort into playing games."

Patrick turned to Dominic, who had since turned away to look at the spectacle of life that played like a movie on a screen. There was something noble in his words, something stronger than the lines in his face would allow.

**

Finding Doug wasn't easy, even though they walked through people and buildings as if they weren't there. Though the air was clear, except for the persistent, gauze-like haze that hung between the worlds, Patrick had trouble making out street signs. Like the murky water of the quarry near the house where he grew up, the air seemed filled with indecipherable particles. They were heavy, like the bug cocoons that floated on the surface of the water, getting in your hair when you came up for air. He could feel the air on his skin; it laid on him like a damp towel. He extended an arm in front of him, as if to brush aside heavy drapes and make way.

Dominic's steps were surer than his. He navigated the haze like an experienced chauffeur behind the wheel of a well-oiled machine.

Patrick gave directions to Dominic, though he didn't seem to need them. It was easier to believe that he was guiding the pilgrimage, rather than being led.

"We're not far now," Patrick called, the distance between them growing as the beginnings of fear slowed Patrick's step. If Dominic heard him, he didn't show it. The cross gabled roof of Doug and Chris's split-level broke through the haze, dispersing it like smoke. Patrick stared at the house in utter surprise, his feet planted and still, his mouth slack. The porch was littered with leaves; the rocker at the far side of the houses glided gently back and forth in the light breeze. Twin pumpkins sat on either side of the top porch step, a playful grin on Chris's, an evil grimace on Doug's - Doug had always leaned to the darker side of Halloween, choosing to be Dracula instead of Peter Pan, the Devil instead of a Fireman. Patrick chuckled at the time he and Joanne had finding a cape that had a lining and was short enough for his 8-year-old frame.

Patrick eyed the white siding and brick front with amazement. His last visit came to mind, filling it up, threatening to spill over and burn him, but he pushed it away. He had to deal with the current, the here and now. Nothing else mattered.

Patrick steeled himself against the image of his son's face crying over his casket. He could see Doug, smart in his tailored suit, as he cried for him, his lips trembling as his emotion spilled out. Patrick couldn't handle the image, couldn't deal with it at all or he was sure it would paralyze him. He breathed deeply through his nose and out his mouth, unaware that with every exhale he uttered, "ok. Ok," like a mantra. After what seemed like forever, he thought he was steady enough to go inside.

Until the door opened.

CHAPTER TWENTY-TWO

It felt like a movie playing in slow motion.

The foyer was dim even though the sun was shining brightly outside. Patrick could see the mirror that hung on the wall facing the street. An ornamented oval, the mirror had been passed down in Chris's family from the 1800s, as was the half moon, maple wood foyer table directly beneath it. The table was accented with a small yellow vase Chris made herself. It was filled with fresh roses with the velvety red petals.

Figures moved beyond the door, felt moreso than seen. He imagined Doug's hand dropping from the alarm panel mounted on the opposite wall. Chris should have been right there saying something to Doug over her shoulder, the red highlights in her brown hair gleaming in the sun. But he didn't see these things. Instead of his son and daughter-in-law, Patrick saw a blackened doorway, growing darker with every second that passed. The sense of foreboding that came over him from the moment they approached the house was suffocating him.

And then it lifted. The darkness that coated the area like a storm cloud went away, leaving the day bright and promising. *Like music,* Patrick thought suddenly, the voice speaking in his mind sounding more like Joanne's than his own.

Patrick hadn't realized his gaze had shifted from the front door until a little voice snapped him back to the world. It was then, when he saw the owner of that tiny voice, when he saw his grandchild for the first time, that the weight of his emotions took over and he fell to his knees.

The little girl — Patrick's granddaughter — inched down the porch stepson her bum, her little legs stretching out toward the next step almost before her behind was planted on the first. Her maroon corduroys were a little too big for her and she positively swam in her wine, hot pink, and purple sweater. The sleeves of purple long johns peeked out at her wrists. When she reached the bottom, she ran to the pile of leaves stacked in the middle of the yard. Patrick hadn't noticed it before even though he stood just inches away from it.

The little girl's laughter was the best thing he had ever heard.

Doug walked past Patrick and toward his daughter. He knelt behind the mound of leaves and watched her with a mix of emotion etched on his face that only parents could understand. It was one of appreciation and of longing, as though the time had already moved on. He soaked up his daughter's happiness, her unabashed glee, and savored it. Soon a pile of leaves wouldn't phase her at all, and Doug knew it. He had to live in the moment, when her desires were as simple as snuggling up with Daddy after playing in the fallen leaves.

"Come on Gabby, let's get your coat." Doug's voice was calm and smooth.

"Noooo," Gabby sang, squatting into the pile of leaves only to spring upward out of them again. Up and down, up and down.

"Yeeesss," Doug sang back as he scooped her into his arms. The leaves dropped from her like water from a tap. "We'll come out in a minute, but you need your coat. It's almost winter!" Doug kissed Gabby on the nose and she wrapped her arms around his neck. Chris, standing in the open doorway, smiled at them as they walked up the steps.

Patrick looked after them, daring not to avert his eyes, not to blink, or they would disappear. Gabby was so beautiful, with her round cheeks and corkscrew hair framing her little face. *An angel, if ever there was one*, Patrick thought.

As Doug mounted the top step, Gabby lifted her head from the crook of her father's neck and looked right at Patrick. Right at him. They stood seemingly suspended in time: a grandfather beaming at his grandchild, and her smiling back at him with love and recognition spreading over her face. Gabby raised her tiny hand and wiggled her fingers at him. Patrick wanted to turn away, wanted to hide himself from view. He didn't want to frighten her. But her eyes, clear and deep, just like her great grandmother's had been, stared attentively at him.

Doug's steps resounded loudly against the wood slats on the porch. As the screen door creaked on its hinges, Gabby giggled and drove a bent forefinger into her waiting mouth.

"What are you laughing at, silly?" Doug asked playfully. Gabby stared at something on the lawn, where they had been playing minutes before.

"You like the way that sounded, huh? The *creeeaaak*," Doug emulated the sound the door made and Gabby turned to look at him as though startled. Doug's smile made her smile and she wrapped her arms around his neck. She cast one last glance at Patrick, who stood rooted in place, unable to move before Doug stepped into the house.

The door to the house closed, shutting out the world and keeping them away from view. Patrick felt as though he had been hit in the stomach.

Things had changed drastically. As he stared at the closed door, he could even see the changes the house had made since he last saw it, since he saw it with eyes that were alive. The wood surrounding the doorframe was starting to show the first signs of rot, the windowpanes could do with a fresh coat of paint. He could see the changes in Doug's face too; the creases in his forehead had sunken in just a little more than they had the last time Patrick laid eyes on him, the suggestion of gray was starting at his temples. And then there was Gabby. Gabrielle. Named after Patrick's own mother. Doug had adored his grandmother. He followed her around, step for step when they got together. He used to love to sit on her lap and listen to her tell stories about growing up next to a cemetery, her voice full of airy suspense, his eyes full of frightened anticipation. She spun the same tale for him every time, only changing the scenery or the names or both with each iteration, but if Doug caught on, he never showed it. He appeared just as rapt as he was the last time. Losing her was hard on Doug, but he found a way to keep a part of her.

Mom, can you see your Dougie now?

Not for the first time, Patrick's eyes clouded over as he stood on Doug's lawn watching the house. He hoped that somewhere, somehow his mother could see Doug, could see Gabby and the tribute her grandson had made to her. He wished he could stand next to her, wrap his arms around her and feel hers around him as they looked at Doug. Being with her would make it easier to be apart from them, to watch them like characters in a movie, to watch life go one without them. But doing it alone was...

Patrick tried to push the thought away and it went begrudgingly, leaving remnants of itself behind, like streaks of blood on a linoleum floor. What was left was an all-consuming sadness. Things changed without him. When he died Chris was only 3 months. It was late summer, and he was thinking about taking Doug and Chris over the Bay Bridge for some crab. He wanted to pull the top of his convertible down a couple more times before the cool weather came in. And then, all of a sudden, it was all over for him. But it hadn't stopped for them. While he talked with Mark his son became a father. While he wandered aimlessly around The Realm that daughter had grown into a little girl who laughed and talked and played. He was reminded of a saying he read in a book, the title of which he couldn't recall: The world had moved on.

Without him.

"Do you want to go in and visit with them?" Dominic asked, his voice cutting through the chatter in Patrick's mind like a knife.

Patrick turned back to the door and stared at it longingly. How he wanted to go inside, to pick up his granddaughter and hug her, to smile at his son, to kiss Chris's cheek. But he couldn't. So, he denied himself anything more.

CHAPTER TWENTY-THREE

Patrick and Dominic walked in silence until returning to the place where they met. It felt as though only a half an hour had passed since he saw his son and granddaughter playing on the lawn, though the sun was lower, and the night's blackness had started to break through the daytime sky. Seeing his family was like a blessing and a curse. His emotions were torn between elation and impenetrable sadness. But that wasn't what had been eating away at him since being in front of the house. The way he felt was the least of his worries.

"Do you think she saw me?" Patrick asked, his voice grave and serious. "I mean, really saw me? Or was she just looking through me?"

"Hard to say," Dominic started, chewing on the words before speaking them. "But it seemed to me like the beaut looked right at you and liked what she saw."

Patrick stopped walking abruptly and Dominic turned to face him. "But how can that be? How could she see The Realm, see us standing there looking at her?" Patrick shook his head, suddenly sorry he every traipsed along The Realm highway and intruded in their life.

"I didn't say she could see The Realm," Dominic corrected with a measured voice and solid eyes. "I said she could see you."

Patrick sighed in frustration, the air coming from the bottom of his lungs to flow hotly over his lips. "How can that be possible?" Patrick breathed. "Unless she…" He couldn't bring himself to finish the sentence.

"As right as you are about that, it isn't the reason she can see you." Dominic's eyes gleamed as though he had a secret he wanted to tell for years and was just about to spill over. "Sometimes children see things adults can't. Animals too. And psychics."

"Are you telling me she saw me as clearly as she saw Doug?" An anger he didn't understand welled inside him, burning his cheeks and thickening his breath.

"Not quite the same, but she saw you nonetheless."

Patrick's silence was enough to coax Dominic into continuing.

"Have you ever seen something in the corner of your eye, the turned to it and there was nothing there?" Dominic continued. "Haven't you ever felt a room grow cold all of a sudden, then warm back up without a source for draft?"

Patrick nodded almost imperceptibly.

"Most people have a brush with The Realm during their lifetime, but they don't know what it is, so they forget about it. But the children, sometimes the old, almost always the dying, and the bastards with the gift, see it for what it is. They can handle the image, aren't afraid of it like the rest of the world would be."

Patrick shook his head in dismay. "It's a curse. That a child should see someone standing in front of her, that isn't really there is cruel."

"Children see the emotion more than the person. To her you probably looked the way you do in the pictures your son shows her. She could feel your love for her and saw you that way. She knew who you were. And she wasn't afraid."

Patrick remembered Gabby's face when she saw him, the light that shone in her eyes, the smile that spread across her face. She *wasn't* afraid. The recognition in her eyes was undeniable.

"To think that I might have frightened her..." Patrick mumbled.

"She didn't see the hole in your chest, "Dominic said, his voice taking on a veil of empathy and kindness. "She saw the face of her grandfather smiling back at her." Dominic looked away for a moment, the emotion he felt threatening to spill over and drop bitter tears on his cheeks. "Would I visit with my sister and her little cherub if I knew it would make them cry?"

Patrick looked at Dominic as though seeing him for the first time. There was a sadness about the man that hadn't shown through his brash exterior. There was kindness as well behind those bloodshot eyes. But there was something else there too. Something Patrick couldn't put his finger on, but it bothered him all the same.

Night draped The Realm like a heavy cloak. Patrick realized distractedly that he was going to make camp with Dominic again, whether he was comfortable with it or not. There was no way he would find the clearing he made the night before, not in the blackness that enfolded them. He glanced quickly at Dominic, stealing a look at the man he happened upon that morning, a man he wasn't sure if he should trust even after everything he had done to help him.

CHAPTER TWENTY-FOUR

"What about these psychics," Patrick asked as they cleared a space for him to sleep. Dominic's frown went unseen in the darkness. "You called them bastards before. Why?"

Dominic rested in the space he would use for a bed that night. He sucked on a twig for a while before answering.

"The psychics are the Hunters of the real world, though most of them don't know it."

Patrick shifted on his makeshift bed of leaves and twigs. "What?"

"They help Mileeha and Mal find the next soul to be taken." Dominic's voice sounded weary. "Didn't your priest tell you that psychics were of the devil?"

Patrick's mother had enlisted the help of a psychic once to read her palm. She had played the lottery and thought it might be fun to find out what was going to happen. When she hit, just like the psychic said, she became paranoid and gave the money away, all $150.00 of it. She said it was evil, the work of the devil. Patrick wanted to ask her why she went to the psychic if all she was going to do was freak out, but he didn't. He figured some questions don't need to be asked to be answered.

"The psychics can see the next person on the list or book or whatever Mal and his buddies have? What, then he looks in his crystal ball and points them out?" Patrick couldn't hide the sarcasm in his voice.

Dominic eyed him curiously. "After everything you've been through, everything you've seen, you still have the audacity to be skeptical?" Sticking his twig back into his mouth, he said, "Seems a bit daft, if you ask me."

Patrick rolled over onto his back and sighed. The stars winked at him from high above, like they had when he used to look at them from his porch. There were different worlds going on about their business, nothing more than shining dots in the sky to us, like Earth was to them. Patrick had never questioned that there was life on other planets. So why did it seem so far fetched that there were seers, ones who knew when people would die, ones who could tell if someone was in the Book of Life or part of Mal's tally?

"So, they work for the Hunters?"

Dominic's voice was thick with fatigue. He sounded as though he had fallen asleep and was clawing his way out of a fog to answer.

"Not exactly. Mileeha works through them to find us. There is a list. There are no names. They find us by looking at our spiritual impression."

Dominic fell silent again and Patrick wondered if he hadn't passed out like a narcoleptic might. He raised his voice and asked, "Our souls?"

"Yes," Dominic replied groggily, but in time. "Our souls never change, no matter how we make ourselves over or change our names. Mileeha shows himself to the psychics and enlists their help. Most of them don't know what they're doing. He deceives them. They think they're helping a lost soul find his family for one last visit. They don't know they're sending the executioner after the prisoner. At least most of them don't."

"But couldn't they see it? Couldn't they tell that harm was coming to the person? I mean, if they are really worth their salt, that is."

"Futures change like the wind. The only sure thing is that a person will die on a certain date at a certain time. How that happens is up to them."

"Up to them?" Patrick asked, suddenly enraged. "Look I don't know about you, but I didn't want to be shot. If I had it my way I would have lived through that day and been there to see Gabby be born." Mentioning his granddaughter's name made his heart ache.

"Yeah, but it wasn't meant to be. Don't you see that yet Patrick? You weren't supposed to see your granddaughter born. You were going to die that day come hell or high water, whether you walked into that house or not. If you decided to take a drive that morning instead, you would have been in a car accident. If you had decided to take a jog, you would have had a heart attack. If you had decided to sit in front of the tele, you would have simply dropped dead. At that same moment, you would have said goodbye to the world you knew and entered The Realm. It was inevitable. It was fate."

Dominic, who had raised onto his elbows and faced Patrick lowered himself back to the ground and closed his eyes. Patrick sat bone straight in the darkness. He replayed all of what Dominic had said about fate, about the inevitability of death, searching for the thing that bothered him. The conversation alone was disturbing, but it wasn't the topic that made him take notice. It was something else.

The house.

Patrick never told Dominic about the house.

Icy cold fear crept up Patrick's spine as realization flooded in.

As if on queue, Dominic said, "Go now. Go before they get too close. Even though they know you're here, it isn't you they want. At least, not yet."

"You son of a bitch," Patrick spat in a hoarse whisper.

"That I am, mate, and worse, I suppose. But that won't save you now, will it? Mileeha can be spiteful and if you hang around here too long you just might learn that for yourself."

The sound was far off in the distance, a good distance away from them, around the mountain and through the valley, but Patrick could hear it, nonetheless. He didn't trust his ears to know if he was right, but he couldn't pull himself away without knowing.

"How could you do it? You've got a niece. You know what it's like. How could you let me lead you right to my family?"

Dominic's laughter penetrated Patrick's mind as though embedded in it. It resonated in highs and lows, echoing off the walls, yodeling, repeating. It took all Patrick had not to crush Dominic's skull with his bare hands. The only thing that stopped him was the sound of the Hunters, their footfalls growing closer and closer.

Dominic's eyes flicked between the road and Patrick nervously while the cynical smile stayed on his lips. "Go now or meet Mileeha face to face and see what he makes of you. Makes no difference to me, but it might to you."

The Hunters' stench preceded them, a noxious mix of bile, licorice, and alcohol; a repulsive musk that screamed of anticipation. Patrick turned away from Dominic and peered through the darkness for a path, a way out, a place to hide. He looked at Dominic once more and said, "I hope it hurts."

"I'm quite sure it will."

CHAPTER TWENTY-FIVE

Lydjauk watched from its perch as Patrick scampered in the darkness, searching for a place to hide. It understood Patrick's need to see what would happen to Dominic; it too had felt the same when it was first betrayed in The Realm. It had no appetite for it anymore, though it felt obligated to stay, like a crowd drawn to an accident clamoring to see something.

Mileeha arrived behind two Hunters, as grotesque in their stature as in their features, pulled in what seemed to be an ancient chariot from the days of the pharaohs. Much of his clothing was from the ancient cultures: a chain mail vestment over his bare torso, a leopard skin sash, pleated metal skirt; a mix match of different cultures and time periods. His death mark was not visible, if he even had one. Most of the Hunted believed he was the son of Mal, immortal like the son of God and of the Devil. They believed that if he walked one earth, he walked all earths, all planets and all times. He was without physical birth and death: he just is. Some believed he was spirit that inhabits the leaders of war, others believe his is the soul reincarnate for every murderer that has and will ever live. No one knew anything for sure, and that made the possibilities of his true nature monstrous.

Mileeha looked Venian to Lydjauk, but looked human to Patrick, his low brow, piercing eyes, and snarled lips clearly those of an African American man. His regal status was apparent in every way including the fact that he wore clothing while everyone else in The Realm was nude.

Mileeha was tall, seeming at first to be the tallest man Patrick had ever seen, but after stepping down from what looked like a chariot, he looked to be no more than six feet. His body was muscular and firm beneath his clothes, which reminded Patrick of armor. His high forehead was capped with silky, dark hair that seemed to glisten in the light. His face was stern and unwavering as he focused on Dominic.

Without so much as a word, Mileeha lifted Dominic from a sitting position to his feet by his throat. At first Dominic appeared to be standing on his toes, straining his neck, elongating his body like a rubber band, but then Patrick saw that Dominic's feet were off the ground and gravity pulled his body painfully toward it.

Mileeha seemed to delight in the pain on Dominic's face, and Patrick was troubled to find that he did also.

Mileeha barked an order to one of the Hunters that sounded more like a grunt than tangible words, and the Hunter lumbered over to them, smelling the air as it went. Fear gripped Patrick as the Hunter first sniffed then looked in his direction. Patrick stood still, hoping the Hunter would turn away, hoping it couldn't make out his shape but knowing it could.

The Hunter toyed with him, staring at the place where he stood for what seemed like an hour before turning its eyes to Dominic.

With the delicacy of a mother handling a child, Mileeha handed Dominic to the Hunter who gripped him with a wart-covered, gnarled, three-fingered hand. The sounds emanating from Dominic's crushed larynx were reduced to squeaks before silencing all together as his windpipe closed. The Hunter stared into Dominic's eyes as Mileeha had, only closer, touching its bulbous nose to Dominic's. From where Patrick stood, they looked like they were dancing, Dominic's legs swaying, kicking, trying to find purchase. And then it seemed that they were kissing, their faces closer together than before. The longer Patrick watched the more the scene changed, the two of them drawing closer and closer, at times seeming to merge flesh with flesh. They turned to face the place where Patrick was hiding, the sides of their heads pressed together, a part of one another. Patrick blinked his eyes to sure it wasn't just his imagination.

It wasn't.

The Hunter and Dominic had become two parts of a whole.

The Hunter's eyes were closed as were Dominic's, and for a moment Patrick wondered if they were both dead. But what was dead in a place where everything had already died somewhere else?

But then Dominic began to move.

His free arm wiggled and jerked, twitching as a dog's leg does during a good belly rub. Then the free shoulder. Then the free leg. His stomach pulsed, rolling like a belly dancer's, waves floating in his and the Hunter's flesh. The Hunter started to wake as well, its body making the same motions as Dominic's had to reengage.

Their eyes opened at the same time.

It seemed a desperate struggle to separate themselves from the other, both Dominic and The Hunter pulling in opposite directions, pushing off each other's momentum. A wet tearing sound made its way to Patrick's ears, turning his stomach. But still he looked. He had to see: he had to know. A gelatinous membrane pulled away from both of their faces; it was the only thing that held them together. Dominic cut through it with a hand that was already beginning to morph into that of a Hunter's; his ring finger had already fallen away, and his pinky dangled by a thread, a bloody ligament that had the elasticity of a rubber band. His skin took on a greenish pallor and warts raised on the surface, covering him in lumpy hills. His hair fell out in one motion, dropping to the forest floor like a wig. The bones in his legs cracked and broke then reformed in the next moment with an odd hissing sound as his height grew 7 or 8 feet. His ribs followed suit, cracking and breaking, puncturing lungs that were too small for his new frame, and melding together again as he grew wide. The Hunter that created him stepped away from Dominic as he completed his transformation, watching with parental glee.

Mileeha's smile was filled with jagged, pointed teeth.

CHAPTER TWENTY-SIX

Lydjauk watched as the creation of another Hunter ended, waiting for the moment when the force field of his curiosity let him leave. Even then, when it was over, he waited for Patrick to leave first; he didn't want to be seen. It wasn't time yet.

Patrick waited until Mileeha, the Hunters, and what had become of Dominic— *He's a Hunter now,* a little voice in Patrick's head admonished, *Better get used to that*— were long gone before moving. He felt like he had been holding his breath forever; the air burned his lungs as he inhaled. He surveyed the area and decided it was best to move on.

Qiao waited until Lydjauk and Patrick had moved far enough into the forest that he could no longer hear their footsteps before moving on himself. Even as the distance grew and the place where Dominic was reborn became blocked and obstructed by hanging vines and tree limbs, Qiao's eyes glistened with fear as much as with wonder.

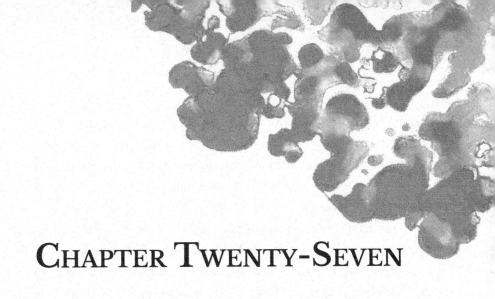

CHAPTER TWENTY-SEVEN

Patrick imagined Gabby in her little corduroys, jumping and laughing in the leaves. He kept thinking of Doug smiling at her as he watched. But then hiss thoughts were invaded by Dominic and the transformation he made right before Patrick's eyes.

Mileeha.

Patrick stood, stretching his legs from the night's inactivity — he had collapsed where he stood when his legs gave out, letting his fatigue choose his camp the night before. The only thing that was important to him anymore was saving Gabby.

Gabby.

The name he so cherished when he heard Doug speak it now haunted him. How could he have led Dominic to her? He felt like he had slit her throat himself! Logic tried to tell him that she was damned to The Realm anyway, that she could no more avoid the curse than he had, but it didn't matter. In Patrick's mind, he had killed Gabby. Unless he could stop it from happening.

As Patrick pushed himself off the ground the feeling of blood rushing to his head was overwhelming. The lifelike qualities he had taken on since death amazed him still, and it was easy to mistake the clever trick as real feeling. With the rush came more images of Dominic, grotesque now in his Hunter state with boils and lesions covering his bloated, misshapen body, taking Gabby, touching her with his rough hands and making her shriek in fear. He saw her kicking and flailing her arms as Dominic held her, dangling her mercilessly off the ground, teasing her with the death that awaited her no matter what she did. The thought of a beast like that touching his grandchild made Patrick weak.

He stood on legs that had numbed beneath his weight. With determination, his eyes searched for the road, for trees that might look familiar, for anything at all that might lead him out of the forest and out into the world beyond The Realm.

With everything he had, he needed to go. Now.

CHAPTER TWENTY-EIGHT

"Jesus, does this guy ever sleep?" Aadi moaned.

"Not after seeing what he saw last night. I'll be surprised if he ever sleeps again," Tara said, her voice thick with sleep. Lydjauk nodded almost imperceptibly, two of its three eyes blinking in Tara's direction.

"How do you know what he saw last night? You were here with us," Aadi said as he stretched and stood.

"Not the whole time. I wanted to see what he was up to." Tara looked first at Lydjauk and then at Qiao. Two of Lydjauk's eyes blinked again — it was pleased at how well she had masked her presence. Though it knew she was there, it hadn't realized it until well into the show playing itself out in front of them had begun. It was Qiao who was surprised by Tara's knowing stare. He turned away, unable to meet it. "I didn't tag along when he visited his family, but I saw them when they got back."

"Them?" Kincaid asked as he sat down next her, crunching leaves loudly underfoot as he did.

"He was with Dominic."

"That son of a bitch!" Sebastian exclaimed, anger tingeing his voice. "That guy deserves to be here. He's a piece of shit if I've ever seen one."

Tara nodded in agreement and continued, "He punched his ticket last night too. He was done for either way. If Mileeha hadn't come for him Patrick would have taken care of it for him." Qiao crept along the perimeter of where the others sat, listening. He was always outside the circle, just out of reach. Tara watched him from the corner of her eye, the same distrust that always crept up in her about Qiao showing its face again. He always seemed sneaky, prepped. It seemed like he was always ready to make a run for it and was just far enough away to have a good head start.

"So, there's another one out there now," Kincaid said, his natural cool taking hold.

Tara nodded again, "One who knows our names and where we camp. So, we need to move. We also need to keep up with Patrick to see what he does. We need to be sure this time," she said and cut her eyes over to Qiao. He saw her but didn't show it.

"Oui, madame," Sebastian said as he bowed deeply from the waist. Aadi rolled his eyes as he stood.

"Let's get going," Tara finished. "Our guy's haulin' ass."

CHAPTER TWENTY-NINE

Patrick made his way back to the street where the living and dead mixed, the former oblivious to the latter's presence, the latter far too aware. He broke through the haze like a rock through the murky glass of an abandoned building, hearing for the first time an audible suction as he did so. He couldn't help but wonder what the people on the street heard, if anything at all. They had no reaction if they did. It was as if people were wearing headphones, blotting out his noise completely.

Patrick repeated the steps he and Dominic took to Doug's house. What if Dominic the Hunter was already there, watching Gabby, biding his time? What would he do? Patrick knew he didn't stand a chance against him. He'd be flattened, ripped apart with just one swing of the hand. The voice of Burgess Meredith rose in his head with stinging clarity, "He'll knock ya till tomorrow, Roc." And then he'd do it again. And again. And again, until Mileeha decided enough was enough - until Mileeha decided whether he wanted another Hunter or a tasty meal.

But he had to do something. He couldn't just let Gabby be killed. Even it if it was her destiny.

CHAPTER THIRTY

Tara peered over hill to gauge the direction Patrick was heading. The barrier between the worlds was denser from the hilltop than it was on level ground and Tara could barely make out the houses and trees that lined the street. Patrick had moved swiftly before reaching the street, but the moment he stepped foot on the sidewalk he slowed. It was familiar to him. And painful.

"Where is he going?" Aadi said, his voice louder than it should have been.

Tara nodded in the direction of Patrick's son's house. She knew. She followed him there the first time.

"Why don't we just go get him? I don't understand why we have to wait so long."

Tara waved Aadi away, ignoring the question and turning back to watch Patrick approach the house. He didn't understand, and she couldn't blame him. No one understood why Patrick was so important to her. They probably thought she was a descendant of his line. That is, everyone but Sebastian. It wasn't true and Sebastian would have known that instantly. He might think Patrick was one of the men she killed on Earth and that she was so interested in him because he would lead the path to Mileeha. That was only half true. As much as Tara wanted to see Mileeha's blood spilled on the barren, decrepit land that was The Realm, she didn't want Patrick to do it, nor did she think he was capable of doing it. She wanted Patrick to lead her to Mileeha – fresh meat was a scent she knew all too well that Mileeha could never ignore. If Patrick got his dander up about something – and from what she saw, he would soon have a hell of a lot to be upset about – the sweet smell of his adrenaline would tantalize Mileeha's nostrils as surely as a steak fresh off the grill would tempt a hungry man. Patrick's anger would lead him to Mileeha's doorstep, where she would gladly cut is throat.

Tara didn't hear Aadi when he left, just like she hadn't noticed the urgent tone in his voice.

"Soon," she whispered more to herself than to anyone else. "When he's ready."

CHAPTER THIRTY- ONE

Patrick stood on Doug's porch and felt the weight of reality pressing on his chest. This house was one of the only places where Patrick felt truly at home. And now all of that was gone.

He had to find Gabby.

The house was dark, the windows like closed eyelids. The silence was almost palpable.

Patrick took another step toward the house, feeling the weight on his shoulders as surely as if he was carrying a load on his back.

He took the steps, pausing only once to look up at the door. He almost expected to see Doug staring back at him, a look of horror etched on his face. But there was no one there. Patrick padded onto the porch with an even stride and walked through the door without slowing. If he had, he would never have been able to go through with it.

The house looked different. Even outside, the siding was a different color and the drapery had been changed to a lighter shade.

Patrick let his eyes rest on the furniture inside, the knickknacks, the artwork on the walls.

Nothing was as he remembered.

How long had it been? Nothing that he saw, not one stitch of furniture, not even the color paint on the walls, looked familiar.

He went upstairs. He didn't notice the pictures that cascaded down the stairwell wall of the new African American family that moved into the house his family had shared, didn't see the picture of the twin boys whose bedroom he would soon be standing in. He was too focused on finding Gabby.

Patrick stood in the doorway of Chris's office and stared uncomprehendingly at the little boys. They were sound asleep, and Patrick was thankful for that, tangled in superman sheets and a blanket was in danger of falling onto the floor. They reminded him of Doug when he was that young. Patrick remembered how, when he would stand in the doorway of Doug's room just to catch a glimpse of him sleeping, Doug would always wake up. It used to startle him, seeing his father standing there. God only knew what those children might think if they saw a man staring at them from their doorway, a man who may or may not be completely solid, and who was undoubtedly a stranger. Patrick moved away quickly and pinned his back against the wall, removing himself from their view in case they woke up.

Where was Gabby?

Patrick hurried to Doug and Chris's bedroom, his mind flooded with worry. How long had he been dead? The question echoed in his head, bouncing off the walls and rebounding to make another pass. How long had it been since he stood in the distance, watching Gabby play in the leaves? What seemed like one night could have been 2 months, a year, ten years on Earth. He couldn't pass through the muddle of fear to find what Bill had told him about time in The Realm. How long had it been since they had met?

Patrick walked through the closed bedroom door and watched the twins' parents as they slept. Their slumber was deep and their breathing was even. Patrick wanted to wake them, to shake the hell out of them and ask, "Where's Gabby?"

Patrick walked down the stairs and out of the house without disturbing anyone inside, his head hung in despair. The one thought he didn't want to have, couldn't allow to take hold no matter what, threatened his sanity again. Had Dominic already taken Gabby?

CHAPTER THIRTY- TWO

Patrick found his way back to camp, his feet moving of their own volition, retracing his steps and bringing him to the place where Dominic died. It wasn't as if Patrick had anywhere else to go.

His mind wrestled with the idea that Gabby had already been taken, that there may be secret portals that would allow passage in or out. But he didn't *feel* anything. Patrick chastised himself for thinking he should, but he couldn't shake the thought. Hadn't his mother and great grandmother felt his presence? Isn't that why they were waiting for him in that in between place before he entered The Realm? How else had they known he was there if not by some instinctual calling? Patrick didn't know but Gabby being dead didn't feel real to him. A little voice in the back of his mind told him that it might not feel real, but it was real.

He had to find Gabby, dead or alive. If she was dead, she would be in The Realm. She would be alone and afraid, like he was. He couldn't bear the thought of a Hunter chasing her. He could almost see her little legs pumping, propelling herself forward, further into the brush while the Hunter toyed with her, catching up and falling behind on purpose, just to smell her fear. He couldn't let that happen.

If she was alive, she was still with Doug and Chris. But where were they?

CHAPTER THIRTY-THREE

Tara looked toward the horizon, her eyes and face blank, as though frozen in death. Sebastian was staring at her and on an unconscious level she knew it—she could almost feel his eyes on her like a bug on bare skin—but she wouldn't pull away from the daydream that had her attention. She wanted to relive her memories, to be a part of them again, if only for a little while.

She was thinking of the time when she and Darren were riding in the Blue Mountains, driving a beaten up convertible through the windy roads. She could almost feel her hair flowing in the cool October wind, could almost see the colorful leaves as they tumbled to the ground and crunched under the tires. She and Darren had stolen that car from an old man in a little town 90 minutes behind them. They had killed him even as he surrendered the keys. Darren had laughed and she felt a flutter in her stomach much like the one she felt when Darren went down on her. But then, as the wind cut through her close-cropped curls and the chill in the air started to lean toward cold instead of cool, she felt remorse. The man hadn't done anything to them. He gave the car up willingly enough, going into the house and coming back with the keys just like he said he would. But Darren said he might have called the cops while he was in there and for that he would need to be punished. And she agreed with him because he knew best. He had been doing this longer than she had and, as he liked to put it, he had a 'taste' for it. So, she agreed with him because there was no reason not to. Darren was right. He was always right.

'Michelle,' he said with his deep voice as sexy as silk and his eyes dipped low in the sunlight, 'I could never let anyone take you from me, baby. No one's ever gonna hurt you 'less they come through me.' That was her name in the life she shared with Darren. She remembered it all like it was yesterday. She remembered feeling like she had heard him say that before, and though she had many times it wasn't the same. She knew Darren was the one who had said before, only he wasn't Darren and she wasn't Michelle. But yet they were Darren and Michelle. She got confused sometimes that way and it was those times when Darren seemed like the most sane thing in her life, even amidst the stealing and the killing. During those times he seemed like he was the only person in the whole world who was truly in control of himself.

Tara remembered that day with Darren just like she remembered others with Jeremy and Ryan, and others whose names were like echoes in her soul. For each Darren there was another Michelle, yet they were all the same. When she found Mitch, she was starting to figure it all out. She was Samantha then and she and Mitch were in Manhattan with the windows down. There was blood on their hands. Mitch was driving fast, weaving in and out of traffic. He was in a hurry to get to the bridge, figuring that once they crossed into Jersey they could relax. She had a flashback in the car that day and she tried to tell Mitch about it, but he threw her off. He gave her the usual line, 'Don't worry baby, you're safe with me'— and pulled her into a tongue kiss like none other before. She hardly had enough time to pull her thoughts together, to hoist them out of the fog induced by his lips before they slammed into the back of a car waiting at a red light. When she opened her eyes, it was to the image of paramedics trying to pull her out of the unrecognizable car. Mitch's body was hunched over the steering wheel, his face bloody and discolored. He was dead; she knew it before she saw the gash on his forehead that was so deep the milky white of bone shone through. But still, as she watched the paramedics pull her lifeless body out of the car, she saw Mitch open his eyes and look at her. One of his eyes was ruined, punctured by glass from the broken windshield. The other eye was terrifyingly clear and focused. Tara remembered feeling rage; a terrible anger that made her want claw the eye out while it watched. The man who possessed that eye wasn't Mitch at all. No matter how coldhearted, how derelict Mitch had been, he could never muster the pure, unadulterated satisfaction that the eye held.

CHAPTER THIRTY-FOUR

Kincaid milled, trying to think of a way to bring it up. Asking Sebastian should be easier than asking Tara, but it was still hard to broach the subject. They had been following behind Tara's lead for days, forever, all told, at least as long as he had been in The Realm. She was the leader of the pack, the self-proclaimed head of their little band of outlaws. No one had questioned her before. There hadn't been a reason to. But this time, as they skulked along the hilltops and hid behind trees, hiding themselves from view from a guy who didn't seem to know his ass from his armpit, Kincaid wanted to know why.

When he was alive, things would never have been the way they were. No woman, let alone a nigger, would have ever told him what to do. He showed them their place before they could even try.

Kincaid remembered seeing them dressed fancy and filing into a dancehall. It pissed him off, their uppityness flaunted like they owned the place. That's when he did it. He took one of those coons walking by and snapped his neck – he could still hear the sound, like a wishbone breaking in two. The girl he was with screamed and came at him, trying to claw his eyes out. He threw her down too and stomped her head into the concrete before anyone could stop him. He heard someone call his name, but ignored it, like he always had. The voice was stern, was angry, was sad. It sounded like his father's the sheriff's, men he'd known all his life, men who'd carried that tone in their voice when speaking his name before. He wasn't sorry and said as much every chance he got. For that they put him to death and when he woke up, he was in The Realm, running for his life. When he met Tara and the others, he almost had nothing left. Tara offered safety, oneness with the group. She called them The Watchers and said they were going to change the way things ran in The Realm as soon as they grew in number. In the meantime, she offered the chance at retribution against the Hunters and he could smell her lust for blood like musk. He tried to put his thoughts about her color behind and had done a good job of it until then. Until he started to feel like he was being led around like a dog.

Sebastian sat with his back to Kincaid and the rest of the group. Lydjauk was off doing his own thing (*probably up in a tree, trying to figure out how to phone home, or whatever fucking aliens do*, Kincaid thought) and Qiao and Aadi weren't around. Qiao rarely was anymore. He wasn't the same as the rest of them. He was more sensitive, softer in more ways than Kincaid cared to count. He didn't understand why Qiao was part of the group – he didn't look like he could protect himself from an ant, let alone a Hunter – but Tara wanted him there and Tara got what she wanted. Always.

Tara was staring off into space and Sebastian watched her from a distance. Kincaid's upper lip twitched as it used to when he was alive whenever he saw black and white people together. It made him sick to his stomach to think that any self-respecting white person would decide to take up with a black person. Sex was one thing, and he didn't begrudge any man that, but marriage? He didn't understand how it could happen. Sebastian would marry Tara if he could. He adored her and had since the moment he saw her, and if you believed what he said, that had been since before they ended up in The Realm. Tara didn't remember meeting him before she died, but Sebastian swore it was her that he knew, her that he had given his heart to. Still, he was her right-hand man and that meant Kincaid had to cozy up.

Kincaid approached Sebastian quietly and sat down beside him. "Nice night, huh?" he said awkwardly.

"Yup," Sebastian said after some delay. His voice sounded as if he were addressing Kincaid from a dream; it was airy and far away.

Sebastian wasn't going to make this easy. Sighing, Kincaid spoke again. "Look, I wanted to talk to you about what we're doing here."

"What do you mean what we're doing?" Sebastian's gaze never left Tara.

"Why the hell are we following this guy around? He doesn't have any skills, hell, he can barely set up camp for himself! And he can't get by the Hunters worth a damn. If we bring him into our group, he'll lead them right to us!" Kincaid's voice came out in a harsh whisper.

"We're following him because Tara wants to follow him," Sebastian said plainly.

Kincaid's anger bubbled over. "Who gives a damn what she wants? Who put her in charge anyway? How the hell does she get final say?"

Sebastian turned to Kincaid and regarded him with colder eyes that he thought possible. "Without Tara you wouldn't be here," he growled. "Don't forget she's the one who picked you right out of the Hunter's clutches. You'd be one of them now if she hadn't saved you."

Kincaid faltered, memories of that day flooding his mind.

"Tara knows why she watches him," Sebastian continued, "She sees more than we do."

"But how?" Kincaid asked, his voice taking on an adolescent whine uncommon for him. "What is she, some kind of psychic?"

Sebastian looked back at Tara. She was up again, on the move, pulled by some unnatural need. "She's more connected to this whole thing than any of us know."

CHAPTER THIRTY-FIVE

Patrick wandered, roaming the city aimlessly, looking for clues. He went to the supermarket, the bookstore, the playground – one he stayed at for quite some time. A little old lady was there with him, as oblivious of him as she was of the cold, nipping wind that made leaves encircle the ground around her feet. Patrick wanted to speak to her, but he didn't. She was looking at a girl riding a swing. Her eyes were so full of emotion, Patrick couldn't bring himself to disturb her. He knew the loss that filled her, that colored her very soul.

Patrick tried the schools in the neighborhood, the libraries, the mall. Nothing. He tried Chris's job, Doug's job. Nothing. He couldn't find their nameplates on any of the cubes. They were gone. It was as if the disappeared into thin air.

Patrick stood in the lobby of Doug's old office building. He was at a loss. The people came on and off the elevators in a torrent, chattering and laughing, noisily ending their workday. But none of them mattered to him.

Where was his family?

Patrick ventured back into The Realm, knowledge tingling beneath his skin like a shock. With only a few steps Patrick traveled the thirty-mile distance that normally took an hour by car and emerged in Washington DC.

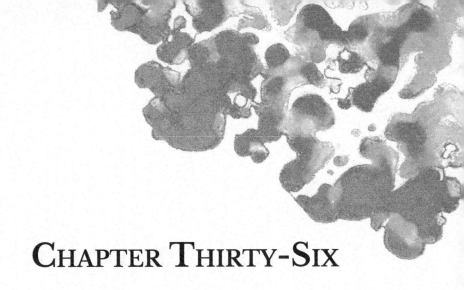

CHAPTER THIRTY-SIX

Tara followed Patrick into the city. It felt good to be around the hustle and bustle, the people walking the streets, the cars speeding by. She missed it. Of everything she missed, this was close to the top of her list. What she missed most she wouldn't allow herself to think of, at least not fondly. She would see it soon — and it would see her.

CHAPTER THIRTY-SEVEN

Lydjauk watched from the top branches of a tall oak as Tara followed Patrick into the city. It had never sampled that particular city but enjoyed the smells and the sounds of Manhattan and of Rome. This one was smaller, quaint as it compared to the others. Washington DC reminded Lydjauk of a place on his planet where Venians assembled and dined. Watching Tara always made Lydjauk feel emotions that it wasn't accustomed to like nostalgia and sadness. And love. That's what Qiao said it was, what he said Lydjauk of feeling. Lydjauk protested when Qiao said it the first time. It overheard him talking with the ever-quiet Aadi. His voice sounded so vile, so contemptuous, Lydjauk almost didn't recognize it. It told Qiao he was wrong, but now, as it watched Tara follow the strange man whom it was sure meant nothing but trouble, it wasn't so sure. It didn't make any sense; Venians didn't experience sadness, love, lust, or any other emotion the way Earthlings did, but the longing it felt when she was gone, the way it warmed when she was near could be nothing other than that.

Love.

And Lydjauk couldn't stop it.

There was something about her, something within her that drew Lydjauk to her. She was evil and dark inside, Lydjauk could see that, but there was also something else. She was sad. Lonely. She ached with it as though it were a throbbing wound. She needed companionship, needed to know that she was cared for. She was searching for it in the most reckless of ways. Lydjauk didn't know what Tara expected from the man she followed and it was afraid that she might not get it. It wished she would see what was right in front of her.

Lydjauk couldn't abandon her any more than it could go back to its planet. The risk to her would be too great.

CHAPTER THIRTY-EIGHT

Patrick had only been there once and that had been years ago, but he remembered the way. He'd made the trek into DC for Joanne because she was worried, had been for days. She said she had a knot in her stomach that wouldn't let up. Patrick asked if it was something about him, or about Doug, but she couldn't say. Or wouldn't. Even when Joanne emerged from the brightly colored, cheery looking place, she looked downtrodden, upset, concerned. Patrick had waited in the car for a half hour watching people walk along the city block, watching the sun dip behind the tops of apartment buildings. It was stupid, he thought. Driving all the way from Maryland to DC for something like this. *At least I'll get dinner out of it*, he remembered thinking until he saw Joanne's ashen face.

"What did she say?" Patrick asked, confusion flashing within him like cold water. He thought the whole idea of going there was to get some assurance, to feel better about whatever was bothering her. Unless...

"What happened? What did she say?" Patrick asked again, spitting the words out in fear. Sudden, cold fear.

Joanne just shook her head, her lips pressed tightly together, her mouth forming a thin line. She looked out of the window toward the storefront she had just left and raised a weak hand to the woman peeking out of the window. Patrick remembered cutting his eyes at the woman, a short, petite Latino woman with a head full of thick, brown hair. He could only see her face for a minute but what he saw soften his stare. It wasn't that she was pretty, because she was. Her face was oval, her lips were full and covered with a pleasant shade of red, an almost ruby color. It was her eyes that made him lighten up. The sadness in them was stifling.

He asked Joanne once more what was wrong, after he had driven out of the city, forgoing dinner for a trip home and hot tea under a blanket in the sunroom. This time she turned to him and said, "It's no use, Pat. Don't fight it."

Joanne was dead ten months later.

The woman with the thick brown hair was starting to pack up and leave for the day. There was an apartment above the shop and Patrick could smell the beginnings of dinner in the air. Garlic and cilantro. The flavors made his mouth water. From outside he could see that not much had changed for her: she still had that beautiful oval face, still wore the same ruby red lipstick. He hoped she would show him the same kindness in her eyes this time.

CHAPTER THIRTY-NINE

Milagros sensed Patrick's presence right away. It was like a cool breeze trickling in from the doorway, moving with him, toward her as he moved. Her back stiffened as it usually did when spirits came around. She never knew if they meant her harm or if they were just lost. The lost ones were easy to handle. They didn't know they were dead, didn't know why they couldn't find their way back home. 'It's not where it's supposed to be', they told her or, 'Someone else is living in my house'. They never knew why they were drawn to her, why they thought she should be able to help them. But she could and she did. Always. She would want someone to help her if she were lost in the afterlife, roaming The Realm looking for something, anything that resembled home. So, she helped them find their way.

The evil ones, the ones who knew what they were and what they could do, were the ones she was afraid of. When they came to her she panicked. They could smell her fear and they relished it. Her grandmother told her not to let them see that she was frightened. She told her that they wanted her to be afraid so they could manipulate her. But she couldn't stop. It was as though she could feel their hot breath on her neck. The easiest thing to do when they came was to get them to leave as quickly as possible. The way to do that was to give them what they wanted. Whatever it was.

This one wasn't lost. He wasn't evil. He was searching for something, or maybe someone. Or maybe both. He was angry, but he wasn't trying to use it as a tool against her. He didn't want to manipulate her, she didn't think. But he wanted something, nonetheless.

"Hello?" Milagros started. She waited before saying, "Hola?" She started to continue in Spanish but decided against it. She didn't think this person spoke Spanish after all. The hesitation she felt had nothing to do with language. It was fear. Confusion. Milagros closed her eyes and tried to feel the being in the room with her. She wanted to read its mind if it would let her. She wanted to know why it was frightened.

"Peter?" She sensed the name. It was like a chalk on a blackboard in its clarity. It had to be his name.

Nothing.

Milagros concentrated again and found another name glowing in the distance. "Jonathan?"

Nothing.

"Martin?"

Nothing.

"Robert?"

Nothing.

"Hay dios mio," Milagros mumbled under her breath. She knew what his silence meant. She dropped into the soft cushioned chaise she used during sessions with her clients and concentrated.

"I'm going to try again, ok? Don't leave. I'll figure this out sooner or later." With considerable effort, Milagros rattled off a two more names before calling out, "Patrick?"

She could feel the composition of the air in the room shift, as it does when a window is opened, and fresh air is let in. "Patrick? Is that it?" Milagros sat up in the chair. She could feel the being tensing, stretching out, reaching for her.

"You can speak to me. I'll hear you. No one else will, but I will."

Milagros thought she lost him. The energy in the room seemed to go still, to gradually reduce until it was gone, as if turned off by a dimmer switch. She started to call his name once more to try and engage him when she felt a presence so close to her it made her recoil. It felt like a cool hand had touched her arm. The feeling wasn't wet and slimy like the touch of the evil ones – how they loved to touch her skin. It wasn't at all unpleasant. Just sudden.

Milagros tried to calm down. She settled back into her chair and waited for Patrick to respond.

"I never thought I'd be able to talk with a living person again," Patrick spoke in a hushed tone he was not accustomed to.

"That's not so hard to believe. Most dead people think that way, that is until they meet someone like me."

Milagros shifted; she could feel him moving around the room.

"None of this makes any sense. I didn't have any problems with anyone. I was healthy." Patrick's mind drifted back to that day.

"You went over to her house, your neighbor, the old woman that lived next door. You went over there because her door was ajar and that was unusual." Milagros closed her eyes and spoke towards the ceiling. Her voice sang the words from her mouth like a long, slow dirge.

"You called for them – her and her nurse – but no one answered. You went inside. You walked through the corridor looking into rooms, still calling for them. But he found you before you found them."

Patrick listened to her speak. He felt as though she spoke to his very soul.

"Mileeha knew you would come. Your kindness is like a beacon to him."

Milagros' eyes opened. She seemed to stare right at him.

"Mileeha? How do you know about him?" Fear returned to Patrick as he put distance between himself and the fortuneteller. How could she know about the goings on in The Realm? The image of Dominic's lascivious leer as he looked at Gabby filled his head.

"He's the one who orchestrated your final day. He's the one who dispatched the Hunter." Her voice was calm and steady.

"The Hunter? What are you talking about? There are Hunters in The Realm but—."

"And they can come into our world also," Milagros said, cutting Patrick off. The smile that spread across her lips was bittersweet. "But you know that. Sometimes we're better off not knowing what goes on around us."

Patrick fell silent. He felt like the wind had been knocked out of him. The fear hadn't dissipated, but it had shifted to allow room for the confusion that bled through.

"Are you telling me that a Hunter from The Realm was waiting for me in Mary's house?"

Milagros closed her eyes slowly; her eyelids were as heavy as a sleepy child's. "Yes," she said finally.

Patrick almost wept, thinking of Mary and Jennifer standing before some beastly incarnation. How frightened they must have been in their last moments. He realized then that he didn't know if they were dead. He never made it far enough into the house to find out.

"Are they—? Did Mary and Jennifer—"

"They are dead, Patrick. They were dead long before you came over to check on them."

A sense of loss washed over Patrick as all consuming as the realization of his own death had been.

"They didn't see what you think they saw, though," Milagros offered. "To them, their attacker was just some guy looking for money for his next fix. They didn't see the beasts you have encountered in The

Realm. The Hunters are shapeshifters; they can assume any form they want in this world and in others."

Patrick's emotions were jumbled together. He was happy they were spared that horror, confused by why his reaction to their fates was strong, intrigued by Milagros' depth of knowledge, and, at the same time, frightened by it. She continued to look in his direction, seemingly right at him.

"How do you know what I am thinking? How can you know any of this?" He wondered how shrill his voice sounded to her ears.

"I can see your thoughts. I can't see the thoughts of the living, but I can read the minds of the dead. Your mind is as transparent to me as it was to Mark. I can see your past, as well as a little bit of your future."

"Can you see me? Standing here right now?" Patrick took a step forward, eager to know.

"Yes, but not the way you were in life. What I see is more like an outline of your former self, like a detailed artist's sketch. I can see the expressions you make; I can see where you are. I couldn't in the beginning because you were wary of me. But your emotion has filled you out, so to speak." A smile played at the corners of Milagros' mouth.

"How do you know so much about The Realm?"

Milagros' face changed from pleasant to pensive. She kicked off her sandals and folded her legs, tucking her feet beneath her. Her eyes fell from Patrick's face and landed on a vase that sat on the table across from her. "They wouldn't have it any other way," she started with great effort. "Just as Arcadia and Abbadon are open to us, so is The Realm. It's the afterlife in total, and though I'd like to be able to block out parts of it, I can't. No true clairvoyant can."

She paused again before continuing, "I can see The Realm and the people there just as well as I can see everyone else. I feel their fear sometimes when they try to escape the Hunters. The Realm lies over this world like a transparency. If the path the person takes goes through my living room, I know about it. Most people will never know anything is going on, but I will. I can hear them crying in the night wishing to see their families who are in Arcadia, wishing to be any place else, even Abbadon."

Patrick's face flushed. She might as well have been talking about him.

"I hear them curse Mal and Mileeha, the Hunters and the cold, bitter nights. And I feel for them." She turned to look at Patrick again. "Your torment is far worse than those in Abbadon. Theirs is only physical. Yours is so much more than that."

Patrick needed to know more.

"What did you mean 'they wouldn't have it any other way'? Who are 'they'? God and the Devil?"

"Neither have a hand in this. You don't exist to them, remember?"

Patrick recoiled, amazed that she could enter his mind and thumb through his knowledge so easily.

"Then who?"

"Mal. And Mileeha, though his reasons are purely sadistic. They wouldn't let me close my eyes to The Realm even if I could. They need me too much."

Patrick remembered what Dominic told him. He was anxious to hear it from Milagros' lips. He wanted to see if the story she told would be the same as his. He wasn't sure what it would mean to him if it were different.

Milagros fell silent. She stared at Patrick, amused.

"Don't you want to know why they need me?"

Patrick shrugged as nonchalantly as he could. "I'm waiting for you to tell me."

Milagros let out a not all together pleasant laugh and sucked her teeth. "Patrick, you have to trust me. If you want me to help you, you have to trust me. No more games, ok?"

Patrick's brow furrowed. "How—?"

"You sound like a broken record! You were going to ask how I knew you wanted help, right? Well, first of all I can read you like a book, I told you that. Second of all, why else would you or anyone be here if not for help of some kind?" Her tone was serious but not angry. "I'll tell you why Mal and Mileeha need me. You are trying to see if I will tell you the truth, and I will, but you have to promise me that you'll stop the games or else you can leave. I didn't lie to your wife and I won't lie to you."

Patrick felt like he had been slapped in the face. He saw Joanne rushing from the very room he was standing in with tears in her eyes all over again. He felt foolish for playing cat and mouse with the woman who was honest enough to tell his wife that she was dying. Patrick nodded weakly. He started to apologize but Milagros cut him off.

"The Realm really isn't as complicated as it seems. It's a lot like here. People use each other for things there just like they do here. Situations are manipulated. People watch each other waiting for their moment to pounce. We are all being watched and being used, even in the afterlife."

Patrick waited for her to continue in silence.

"Mal uses me to find people like you when your lives are up. We don't want to help him, but he is unlike anything you can image. Mileeha doesn't hold a candle to Mal; he doesn't have a fraction of his powers. Mileeha takes his direction from Mal. Mal takes direction from no one. He can be as benevolent as God and as evil and Satan. He can save your life or feed you to the Hunters. And he won't wait for you to die to get you. He will dispatch a Hunter from The Realm to take you kicking and screaming into the afterlife and do with you what he will. Because we can't save ourselves, we help him, knowing that in the end, our resistance would be futile. The fates of the ones we would try to save are already written on the pages of his book."

"His book?" Patrick asked.

"Much like the Book of Life that God holds, Mal has the Book of the Condemned. Mal knows when each person whose name is written in the book will come to him. What he doesn't know is how they will die and he relishes devising interesting deaths for them. Sometimes he has them butchered by madmen, sometimes he has them crushed by cars. But they always die by someone else's hand. They are always murdered."

Patrick sucked in air, feeling his nostrils flare as he took it in. He needed to know more but he was trying to process what Milagros had already told him. Anger welled inside Patrick, replacing the fear. He started to ask Milagros about the relative, that bastard who damned him and his family to a The Realm after death, but another question tugged at him.

"What did you mean when you said our 'lives were up'?"

Milagros gazed at Patrick long and hard before speaking. "That's why I called you by so many names earlier. Peter, Jonathan, Martin, and Robert are names you've used in your past lives. Wallace and George also."

"Past lives?" Patrick cut in, unable to hold his tongue. "What kind of bullshit is this?"

Milagros regarded him in silence, waiting for him to calm down.

"I told you I wouldn't lie to you and you promised you wouldn't play anymore games. What I'm telling you is the truth. It's the piece of the puzzle your friends never told you, probably because they don't understand it themselves. You have to understand that the information you knew before coming in here was what Mileeha wanted you to know. He wants you to be aware of yourself and of what is going on around you. How do you think you've avoided the Hunters so well until now? Surely not because you outran them. You are being protected. Your role in this is bigger than being food for the Hunters. You are meant for something more and even I can't tell what it is yet."

Patrick's head was spinning. He wondered why the Hunters seemed to let up on the chase when a common dog would have downed him and torn him apart. And Bill and Dominic's appearances seemed coincidental now that Milagros pointed them out. He wanted to know about this role she foresaw, wanted to know about the book and if a name could be erased from it. He wanted to know everything she knew all at once.

"The past lives are real. It's your way into The Realm," Milagros continued. "In your first life you committed a heinous sin. Murder. Instead of letting the Devil take you, God brought you back and gave you the chance to set things right. He did this seven times for you, just like he did for every first generation that ends up in The Realm. He figures that if you are coerced to commit a crime, you deserve a chance to repent. So, in six of the seven lives you are allowed to live as long as you did the first time in the hopes that you will repent the sin of murder even if you never commit it again. There are clues given along the way that something might be different about you: you are attracted to the darker side of life, indulge in fetishes, lack of faith — it could be anything. Some people figure out God's plan and run to him, others, most if the truth be told, never do. In their seventh life they are allowed to live three-quarters of the time they lived in their other lives before God throws His hands in the air and gives up. That's when Mal steps in. Your name is permanently recorded in his book just before your lives are up. He sends a Hunter to end your life here so you can begin life under his rule."

Milagros' face looked pained.

Patrick felt himself sliding to the floor. He could feel the wall against his back and floor underneath him when he made contact. He searched his mind, tried to remember something, anything that he might have done.

"It's useless," Milagros said, her voice heavy. "If you couldn't remember it then, you won't remember it now."

"Do you know?" He sounded both hopeful and terrified.

"Yes." Her voice was no louder than a whisper.

Patrick wasn't sure he wanted to know what he had done. To hear about a murder committed by his own hands was like taking a knife to his own neck. He couldn't image having done something so terrible. He didn't want to hear the words spoken aloud.

They sat in silence for a while, him on the floor brooding over what Milagros said, her in her overstuffed chair, watching him. Headlights from a passing car lit the room, calling Milagros' attention away from Patrick. She stood and turned on the lights, then made her way to the kitchen. As she ran water for tea, Patrick spoke.

"Bill told me that someone in my family landed me in The Realm." His voice was weary and drained, but there was something else too. It was coarse. And it was accusatory.

"He said that the relative might not even be there for all he knew. That what the guy did was bad enough that he might be in Hell, but that the rest of his family line was condemned to The Realm. So, what you're saying can't be right. It can't be me."

"Patrick, I know this is hard to believe," Milagros said as she set the teapot on the burner to boil the water. "Mark and Bill told you what he was supposed to tell you."

Patrick couldn't hide his surprise.

"He was manipulated," Milagros added quickly, sensing the feeling of betrayal that engulfed Patrick. "He was overwhelmed with a desire to get to you first, a need to tell you what he could without getting himself in trouble, and most of all to meet his brother for the first and last time. He didn't mean to mislead you. Mileeha planted the suggestion in air and he breathed it in."

Patrick took in Milagros' words, let them turn over in his mind and soon felt better. He couldn't deal with the idea that his brother had betrayed him, that maybe his mother had, and hid his great-great grandmother. He had to trust someone in all of this. If that was taken away from him, he didn't think he'd be able to keep it together.

"Most of what Mark said is right," Milagros continued, "but there is just enough wrong in there to skew your perspective. Dominic shared stories with you that were true too, but not everything, as you found out yourself. He also told you that you would be able to 'see things' about people yourself after you've been in The Realm a while, didn't he? You can't see anything now and you never will. Death doesn't make you psychic."

Patrick was beginning to feel foolish.

"The reason Mileeha had Bill tell you that there was some mystery relative that did this to you is because Mileeha wants you angry. He wants you to come to him for some reason. And you will when the time is right."

Patrick thought of the house he noticed at the clearing near where he and Bill camped for the night. He realized then that it had all been orchestrated. He felt silly, naïve. Moreover, he wondered why he was so special that he was to go to Mileeha. There was more that Milagros wasn't saying. If Mileeha wanted him, all he had to do was send for him.

"Maybe you should tell me what I did."

"Patrick–." Milagros' cautioned.

"I have to know," Patrick rasped. "I have to know how I condemned my family to The Realm."

Milagros poured the boiling water over an herbal tea bag and brought the cup with her to the overstuffed chair. She blew over the tea to cool it and took a sip. When she finally spoke her voice was low, faint, as though it pained her.

"You killed twenty-three people, two of them pregnant women. Pregnant with your children." She glanced at Patrick over the lip of her mug. He looked stricken.

"You impregnated seven women and decided to keep five of them. You let them go, but made the others stay. They watched as you slaughtered people one by one as they came in, cutting them with knives and pieces of broken glass."

"I killed the mothers of my children?" Patrick was overcome with grief. He sobbed so loudly Milagros thought clairvoyants blocks away could hear him. "Why would I do something like that? How could God show mercy on someone like me? I should have gone straight to Hell."

Milagros' face showed sincerity and kindness. She felt sorry for him. Patrick hated her sympathy – he didn't feel like he deserved it. He was disgusting. A killer! A murdering bastard who had no regard for human life. He felt sticky, dirty, as though the blood of his victims covered his skin.

"God gave you a chance to repent because he loved you," Milagros continued. "You were one of his prized humans. You brought his message to the masses. You introduced him to those that were blind to him."

Confusion stood on Patrick's face like stagnant water.

"You were a holy man."

The walls closed in on Patrick. His heart felt like it was going to break open in his chest. A servant of God. A teacher pledged to love humanity. How could he take a life?

"You lost your faith when a young parishioner died during your service. You lay with a woman that night and, in her face, you saw that child laughing at you. You suffocated her there, in the bed where you lay. And then you never stopped. You killed the nuns that lived in the nunnery beside the church, running through all fourteen of them as they came, one by one, to tend to the church. You killed parishioners as they came to worship. You killed the priests who lived with you, who prayed with you, as they slept. But God still loved you.

"He told you that He would offer you salvation if you repented, but you wouldn't. Not in the first life or any of the lives that came afterward, and He gave you vision into your sins in one of them. He told you that He would condemn your family to The Realm if you ignored His Hand, but you never took it. So, all your descendants have been cast to The Realm, as your son and granddaughter will be. As everyone who descends from you will be."

Patrick's head felt full, congested. He heard everything Milagros said, but found it hard to believe, yet impossible to ignore. He kept seeing Doug's face as a baby, in Little League, on his wedding day. He thought of Gabby and her round little face. They deserved eternal life, not to be sent to a place where they have to run for their lives forever. But he did this to them. Him. No one else. He couldn't lay the blame on the shoulders of his father or grandfather or better yet, some relative he had never even met. The horrible truth lay with him and him alone. It made him sick.

With marked difficulty, Patrick asked, "Is there nothing I can do to change this? Doug and Gabby don't deserve this. Can't I just go to Hell and pay for my sins?"

Milagros smiled ruefully, "It's not as simple as that. You can't just move to Hell and spend eternity suffering there. The punishment is different. It is physical in Hell. The worst torture is administered and when you are on the brink of death, you start all over again… forever. Though that sounds bad, what The Realm has to offer is far worse. There the punishment is mental. Sure, there are some physical aspects. As prey you have to run and hide, never sleep, always be on your toes forever. But in The Realm, you are damned to run across your relatives, none of which did anything of their own to be there."

Milagros sighed. "God can't see you anymore, Patrick. Neither can the Devil. To them, you don't exist. You belong to Mal now. And no one escapes Mal."

Milagros took a sip of tea. Her nerves were shot. This kind of news was bad. She never knew how they would react.

"I have to save them," Patrick mumbled under his breath. His mind toggled between Doug and Gabby, their smiling faces, the way Doug looked when he slept. His reason for coming flooded his mind then, washing away the images of Doug and Gabby and replacing them with red-hot panic. Patrick asked,

"Can you see my family? My granddaughter Gabby —I think they're coming for her."

Milagros nodded and said, "I can see them, yes."

"I need to know where they are. I went to the house and a new family lives there. I have to find Gabby. I have to do something to keep her safe."

Milagros started to tell Patrick there was nothing he could do, that her lot had already been cast, but she thought that might be like rubbing salt in an open wound. The look on his face, the pain in his eyes told her that even if he knew her words were true, he would still try to save her. And what harm could it do? Death wasn't a risk; he had already crossed that threshold. Mal and Mileeha obviously had plans for him, or else, she doubted he would still be alive.

"They moved the next town over. To Herndon," Milagros said, traveling the distance from their old house to their new one in her mind. "But the house is smaller... and Doug doesn't live there anymore."

"What?" Patrick said, alarmed. "What do you mean Doug doesn't live there?" He almost couldn't form the words. "Is he... dead?"

"No, no, he's not dead. He just isn't there anymore. He lives in DC. Downtown, near The Mall."

Patrick stood confused, trying to process what she was saying. "You mean they've separated? Have Doug and Chris separated?"

Milagros took another sip of tea. "Yes."

"Where is Gabby?"

"In Herndon with her mother."

Patrick sighed and searched the ceiling for answers. Things seemed to have turned upside down over night. A question came to him and was out of his mouth before he could fully form the thought, "How long have I been dead?"

Milagros didn't know how to handle that question. It was an easy answer, but after everything she had told him already, it might be enough to send him over the edge. She contemplated stalling, sipping her tea, pacing the room, anything to buy more time, but she knew that was too obvious. She looked at Patrick. He was a kind man in his last life, she knew. It was that persona that controlled the entity now, not the holy man or the wife beater that came before it. She decided to give him a straight answer.

"Thirteen years."

It seemed like all the air had been sucked out of the room.

"Do you know what—?" He didn't know if he should ask. It felt like invasion of privacy somehow.

"There's a woman with him," Milagros started.

"Oh God," Patrick groaned.

"They aren't living together, but she's with him now."

Patrick was furious with Doug. He was ashamed of his son's behavior. He had broken up his family to be with another woman. The anger sweltered behind the concern for his granddaughter.

"Tell me where Chris and Gabby live. I need to see if Gabby's all right."

Milagros told him where to go. He knew the place. It was right behind the old farm that the community surrounding it was named for: Franklin Farm.

"Milagros," Patrick said with honest sincerity, "Thank you for everything. For me, for Joanne. I wish I had thanked you when I was alive but..." His voice trailed off.

Milagros sat silently in her chair. She didn't know whether to stop him or let him go. There was nothing out there for him, nothing that he could do, but he had to go. She knew it like she knew when Joanne was going to die. Her confusion left her tongue-tied and quiet.

Patrick looked at the woman who had read his lives, who had given him a roadmap to his family, and wondered what cost she would have to pay for her kindness. The thought brought shame with it and he found he could no longer look her in the eye. With an almost imperceptible nod, he left the room, traveling through the door the same way he entered.

As Patrick left, Milagros wondered how long it would be before Mileeha paid her a visit.

CHAPTER FORTY

The smile that spread over Mileeha's face was brilliant, as beautiful as it was horrific. His eyes glistened as the future played out before him, just the way it was supposed to.

Mal, from the dark corners of the house that he and Mileeha shared, reached for Mileeha's thoughts and found red, but it wasn't the sentiment of slaughter that filled his mind. Lust saturated his thoughts and blurred the edges of reality and memory. In Mileeha's red-hot musings Mal found many names, but only one that rang true. He grabbed the name in his own mind, a place the likes of Mileeha, the devil, nor God Himself could enter, and encircled it with a massive hand, entombing it in an impregnable vice.

Chapter Forty-One

Patrick used The Realm to cover ground, making his way to Franklin Farm in a matter of minutes after leaving Milagros' store. His head was pounding like it used to when he'd had too much to drink (sometimes Patrick hated the realism The Realm offered. Some things were best not relived.). He tried to make sense of what happened, but it was too much to bear. He loved Chris like she was his own child. The whole thing tore him apart.

Franklin Farm was a nice enough area, filled with single-family homes and paved sidewalks with tons of children and dogs. The trees were tall and full, unlike the newer communities with trees were nothing more than saplings, their leaves nothing more than buds. The street that Gabby and Chris lived on was similar to all the others. It gave him a homey feel, like his old street used to. Homesickness washed over him in a torrent and he fought to hold it at bay, knowing better than to think he could force it away all together.

They lived in a corner townhouse. The bright red door in the center of delicate canary yellow siding hinted at the house's character. Patrick could see why Chris liked it all ready.

The inside was bright and airy with light-colored walls and neutral furniture. He saw Gabby at different stages in her life and marveled at how beautiful she was. It registered with Patrick that there were no pictures of Doug around.

That Chris had bought new furniture troubled him.

Patrick went upstairs first. It was around lunchtime and Chris' car was in front of the house. He thought maybe they were upstairs in their rooms. When he went up the stairs, he smelled Chris's perfume in the air. Sunflower. She had always been partial to that scent, ever since Joanne had given it to her on her first Christmas in the family.

Patrick looked in the other bedrooms and didn't find anyone. The rooms were painted white and there was hardly any furniture. Chris was using one of them as an office with a desk, computer and printer crammed into a corner as if she was trying to conserve space. There was nothing else in the room. The rooms — the house — were like bare skeletons compared to the house Chris and Doug shared. Seeing them that way made Patrick's heart hurt.

He went into Gabby's room last. Her walls were covered with posters of boys: boys by themselves; boys in a band; boys in cars, all of them striking a pose they thought was sexy. Patrick guessed that to a young girl they were. A desk stood in the far corner, covered with textbooks and pads and dirty clothing lay in a pile next to the bed. It hit him hard, like a slap in the face. He expected to see toys stacked in the far corner of the room and a canopy bed adorned with a frilly comforter and stuffed animals, not the chaos of a teenage girl. But that's what Gabby was. A teenager. It had been thirteen years since he had last looked in on her. To him it seemed like only a day ago.

While Patrick's eyes cascaded over Gabby's things, he wondered if she still called herself Gabby or if she preferred the more mature

Gabrielle. He hoped she could see her great-granddaughter. She would be so honored to have a namesake (she had always hoped that he and Joanne would have a girl). Patrick shook his head as tears threatened to spill over his eyelids.

Gabby was growing up so fast. He had missed everything – her first day of school, her first gold star, her first crush. Everything. He knew he was dead, but at least he could have seen some of it from The Realm. But he hadn't been watching. He hadn't been there spiritually, just like he wasn't there for her in the flesh.

Something caught his attention on the other side of the bed. A mound of clothes covered it, but he could still make out what it was. Panda! Panda was propped up, its back against the wall across from the bed. He had given Panda to Doug when he was a baby. The panda was massive with a large round head that was at least two times the size of any adult's and a body even bigger than that. Doug used to lie in Panda's lap when he was a baby, used him as the host for his imaginary friend when he was five, and as a clothing rack (like father like daughter) when he was seven. Patrick had always hoped Panda would be able to come out and play again. His wish had come true.

He found them in the basement.

Chris and Gabby sat in the middle of the floor working on a collage. Gabby worked slowly, cutting the tracing paper and picture in the shape while Chris waited to apply glue to the back of it. A big piece of foam board laid waiting, propped against the sofa.

Relief ran through Patrick as he stood and watched mother and daughter wile away a Saturday afternoon. Gabby looked fine, healthy. There was nothing hovering around her, waiting for the right moment to strike. At least he didn't think there was. The air in the room was as temperate and as calm as it should have been. No Hunter shape-shifted into a person stood waiting in the shadows. As Patrick thought this, his eyes focused harder on Chris. Could she be a shape-shifted Hunter? He didn't think so. Her eyes looked the same as they always had, bright and clear, and a beautiful shade of brown. Her smile appeared genuine as she watched Gabby cut out her shape, not conniving and devious. She was older, the lines around her eyes and mouth told him that. But she was still Chris. Beautiful, vibrant Chris. The same, if not a little wiser and weather worn. When Chris laughed at the odd shape that Gabby finally carved out – in the end it looked more like a donkey than anything else – Patrick knew he was right.

With a sigh of relief, Patrick watched a while longer, enjoying his time with Gabby. He wished he could touch her, hug her, tell her how much Grandpa loved her. But he didn't dare. He feared that if he indulged just one of those fantasies, she might see him and be frightened. That was the last thing he wanted to do. Reluctantly, after untold time and while Chris took a nap on the sofa and Gabby talked on the phone, Patrick left. He would come again to see her, he knew. He didn't think he could stay away.

The sun dipped behind the houses and the night sky slowly but surely covered the brilliant red, oranges, and mustard yellows of sunset with magenta, then plum, then navy. Patrick walked the streets of Chris and Gabby's new community, deciding not to use The Realm until the midnight blue sky had taken over all of the other colors. He mourned the breakup of his little family. He was angry with his son for being with another woman. He pined for his granddaughter's smile. The mixture of emotions was intoxicating.

Doug.

He needed to see Doug.

Patrick wanted to give Doug a piece of his mind. He wanted to know why he did it. Joanne used to say that Doug and Chris were just like they had been when they were young. In love, about love, and love itself. She called them soul mates and Patrick agreed. He couldn't have imagined Doug with anyone else.

And now all that might be over. Probably was already over.

Without consciously thinking about what he was doing he headed towards the city again. He was going to find Doug, was going to talk with him if he could do it without scaring him to death, and he needed Milagros' help to do it.

CHAPTER FORTY-TWO

Milagros felt him.

Like hands on her skin, hot with passion, she felt him. She turned to face him only to find there was no one there. He was playing with her and it frightened her.

He only played games when he was angry.

Mileeha hid just beyond Milagros' vision in the land where all creatures bowed to him, save for one. His white teeth gleamed in the darkness. They would be the first things she would see. He hoped it might make her look at him in desire instead of fear. Her eyes might soften and she'd sit with her legs folded in front of him, offering a glimpse of thigh. As busy as he was, taking her might have to be fit into his schedule after all.

Milagros searched the room, her pupils widening and shutting as she peered through the dimly lit room. By the time she saw Mileeha his smile was attached to a tall, virile, man's body. *He is nice to look at,* Milagros thought not for the first time. The outline of his features lent much to the imagination. But those good looks, those piercing eyes, that man was anything but nice. One doesn't get to be the right-hand man of the Devil's brother by being nice.

"Mileeha," she said softly.

"Milagros," he replied. His voice was satiny and disarming. She hoped her fear didn't show on her face.

Mileeha stared at her in silence for the better part of a minute. His intense gaze scared her, and that was probably good. Her fear would keep her in line. Her fear would stop him from having to hurt her.

"Who did you speak to today, Milagros?" Mileeha sat. It was a human action, one that would disarm Milagros. He enjoyed playing with her mind as much as he enjoyed watching the Hunters chase their prey.

"I had a couple of customers," Milagros started as she took a seat in a chair close to his. She knew better than to sit too far away from him; she had felt his lustful eyes coursing over her body enough times to know that he enjoyed her. She knew better than to try and run. He was already inside her head and there he would remain no matter how much distance she put between his physical body and hers. He wanted answers and he would get them. No matter what.

Mileeha nodded as though interested in her niceties. She was taking in deeper breaths than she had been before, though trying to hide it. The rise and fall of her bosom restrained him from cutting to the chase.

"Interesting customer? Did he find his lost love, or did you give him the winning lotto number?"

"He was looking for his family, so I showed him where to find them." She didn't know what else to say.

"But that's not all you did, is it?" Mileeha leaned forward to look her in the eye. The fire that gleamed in his own sent a chill down Milagros' spine. "Tell me, what could have kept Patrick here so long, and after hours, no less?" He smirked. "It must have been some tale."

Milagros shifted in her seat, knowing Mileeha was enjoying every minute of her discomfort.

"I told him that his son was having an affair and that he and his wife had split up. I showed him where to find his granddaughter and how she had changed since he last saw her."

Mileeha let the silence sit between them. He watched her as she shifted in her seat, sitting on one hip first, then moving to the other, all the while hoping he didn't notice. Her anxiety was palpable, and as sweet as fruit from the vine.

"There's more, Milagros" Mileeha hissed. "Much, much more. Isn't there?" He paused for effect. He saw fear flash across her face and smiled, satisfied. He continued, "You told him about The Realm and how he got there, didn't you?"

Milagros felt heat on her neck as though hot water beat against it. She had to tell him the truth; there was no other way around it. He already knew.

"Yes."

Mileeha sat back, his expression unreadable. "Why? What made you tell our little secret, and to someone you don't even know, Milagros?"

"The afterlife is no secret," she said, more defiantly than she had intended. "We all have to find out for ourselves when the time comes."

"Some will learn sooner than others."

Milagros froze.

"He's coming back here. You know that don't you?"

She hadn't thought about Patrick since Mileeha showed up. She searched for him in the haze that allowed her to see both worlds and saw him approaching the shop, not two minutes away from her door.

"Yes."

"I want you to tell him what he wants to know. He can't stop it, but the poor fool doesn't know that yet." Mileeha rose to his feet, standing his full height. Even though he wasn't close to her, she could feel him standing over her, looking down into her soul.

"Tell him what he wants to know and maybe I'll let you live." His words lingered in the air like mist.

Milagros was terrified, more frightened than she had ever been in her life. Her mother had been a fortuneteller also and had told her of evil spirits coming through and manipulating clairvoyants. She herself had been possessed for an hour or two by a wife who was angry that her husband had married his sister not two weeks after her death. She tried to use Milagros' mother to kill her husband, but she was too frail to go after her. It took another clairvoyant to talk the woman out of Isabella, begging her to leave before she killed her. Milagros had no illusions about what could happen. She knew what could happen if those dwelling in the afterlife, whether Abbadon, Arcadia, or The Realm, could do to her. She knew Mileeha could kill her with the flick of his wrist.

"Do you understand me, Milagros?" Mileeha challenged. "I will take you to meet your maker before you finish your sentence if I you disobey me. And you might be surprised to find out where you end up."

Mileeha's last comment was enough to make her pass out. She had a strong urge to mark the sign of the cross on herself.

The door to the shop seemed to melt, to become liquid as Patrick passed through. Just like before, it returned to solid after he was inside the room. Milagros searched for Mileeha's aura in the room and found nothing.

CHAPTER FORTY-THREE

"I found Gabby," Patrick started as soon as he entered the store. "She's fine. She's more than fine. She's… thriving." Patrick couldn't help smiling.

"I'm glad." Milagros didn't know if she should prod him or let him ask her what he wanted to ask. All she knew was that she wanted it to be over.

"I need to see Doug," Patrick said. There was something different about Milagros, something distant. He didn't know why he would notice something like that, why he would care at all. But he did notice.

"Doug?"

"My son. I need to see him now."

Milagros saw the scenario as plain as day for the second time. Mileeha was right. It was already too late. Patrick couldn't do anything to help Doug even if he had made it there before the wheels were set in motion. He and his family were damned to life in The Realm and there was nothing that could be done to reverse it. She started to tell him that but the thought of Mileeha silenced her.

"I need to see him, Milagros. Please, tell me how to get to him?"

"What are you going to do if I tell you? It's not like you can speak to him. He's not clairvoyant."

She could feel the heat on her neck.

Patrick hung his head. She had a point. No matter how much he wanted to show himself to Doug, no matter how much he wanted to give Doug a piece of his mind, he couldn't. Doug had never shown any signs of having a sixth sense or being able to see things in the future. With his shoulders slumped, Patrick said, "I don't know. I just really need to see my son. I've seen my granddaughter and now I want to see Doug."

There was nothing Milagros could say to dissuade him; she knew that before he left the first time. She didn't know what giving him the information was going to bring — she could only see as far as Doug's death — but she gave it to him anyway. Maybe that was really all Mileeha wanted from her. Even before she finished that thought, Mileeha's laughter filled her head.

"The woman is still there with him," Milagros said as Patrick turned toward the door. Patrick turned back to her and smiled thinly. "Thank you," Patrick said. "I'll try not to bother you again."

Milagros nodded as he turned his back on her and left the shop. She didn't think he'd be back, not because he wouldn't need her help anymore, but because there wouldn't be a shop for him to come back to.

CHAPTER FORTY-FOUR

The place was easy to find. It was in the middle of the city, off Pennsylvania Avenue. Patrick followed the directions Milagros gave him and found himself in front of the building before he was ready to be, before he knew what he planned to do. He mounted the steps, climbing them instead of hovering above them, as he knew he could, wanting to feel the texture of the stairs beneath his feet. He needed to clear his head. He needed a plan.

Patrick stood in front of Doug's door thinking of what he would say to his son if he could. The door was dingy, as was the building. Old, with cracked paint on the ceiling and rusting handrails. *Doug must be down on his luck*, Patrick couldn't help thinking. He couldn't help but feel sorry for him.

Patrick walked through the door the same way he had walked through the door to Milagros' shop, feeling the metal rippling around him, rolling over him like warm water. He found himself looking at a room that was threadbare and unadorned.

Patrick didn't have very far to go to find them. The bed was pressed against the far wall of the studio apartment, on the other side of a card table. Doug was on the bed, his new lover lying next to him. They were naked, sleeping on top of the sheets, their bodies entwined leg over leg. It made Patrick sick.

"You stupid son of a bitch!" Patrick yelled at Doug, giving it everything he had.

Nothing.

Doug didn't even stir in his sleep.

Sadness rushed over Patrick and he staggered. Doug couldn't hear him — of course he couldn't! Patrick used to belief those ghost stories he heard growing up, at least half-heartedly. Ghosts carrying candelabras or knocking paintings off the wall. But he knew now that those stories were completely made up. He could even knock down a coffee mug in his current state.

Patrick wished he had never come. He didn't want to see Doug like that, living in squalor and holed up with some cheap trick he found to fool around with.

The woman — the cheap trick, as she remained in Patrick's mind — was looking at him.

Right at him.

Seeing him.

Patrick jumped, surprised. She saw him, to truly see him like he was alive. Patrick looked back at her, surprise etched on his face.

Then she smiled at him.

Patrick stumbled backwards, fear chilling his body. He realized, with distracted amusement, that he could feel goosebumps rising on his skin. The woman raised her head first, then her torso off the bed, moving with a spider-like quality that made Patrick's skin crawl. She never took her eyes off him.

"Who are you?" Patrick whispered, afraid that Doug might hear him. Afraid of who else might hear.

The woman laughed, but the sound was more like a violin that needed tuning. Patrick recoiled as if slapped.

"What—," Patrick started, but the woman turned away from him, focusing her attention on Doug instead. Doug slept quietly, unaware of the woman's movement. She caressed his face with what looked like a loving gesture until Patrick noticed thin swirls of blood rose on Patrick's skin. He rushed forward but could gain no ground. The woman put her lips over Doug's and kissed him. In his sleep, Doug opened his mouth, receiving her tongue, which had changed from a natural pink to a poisonous black before it slithered into his mouth. She ran her hands along his chest, leaving streaks of blood behind.

"Stop it! Stop it!" Patrick yelled. The woman lifted from her kiss and looked at Patrick once more. The tone of his skin had changed from a caramel brown to an iridescent Hunter green. The color of the Hunters. The sacks that floated on its skin seemed to pulse, seemed to rise and fall as if wanting to be touched. What was perhaps most disturbing of all was its face. On top of the heinous Hunter's body sat the beautiful head of a girl with brown skin and oval light green eyes. It grinned at him with a mouth full of jagged teeth.

"Doug!" Patrick called out, trying to will his son to wake up. Nothing.

"God help me!" Patrick yelled, his head upturned to the ceiling of apartment. The Hunter laughed even louder than before, its body writhing on top of Doug. The movement made Doug stir and finally awaken. His scream called Patrick back to the situation.

"What the fuck?" Doug yelled, shock and fear mingling together to thicken his voice. "Gina?"

Patrick saw the pain on Doug's face and cried openly. He could only imagine what was going through Doug's mind. Seeing something like that, on top of you, was enough to drive a man crazy.

They can see you when they're on their way out. That's what Mark had said. Patrick was afraid, but he had to know.

"Doug?"

Doug's eyes were opened painfully wide as he stared at the monstrosity lying on top of him. The thing that used to be Gina was smiling at him with teeth that looked as sharp as razors. Her body was like no animal he had ever seen. It seemed to enjoy his fear.

Then he heard his name.

Not only his name. He heard *his father* calling his name.

"Dad?" Doug said, his voice shaking. He couldn't pull his eyes away from the thing straddling him. "Dad, if you're there, help me!"

Doug hadn't believed in ghosts before, but he was ready to believe anything now.

Patrick tears stung his eyes. He tried to run for the bed again, his arms outstretched. He was going to pull the Hunter off Doug and kill it if he could. He wanted to save his son from being condemned to The Realm. He just needed more time.

Patrick's legs felt as if they were glued to the apartment floor. He couldn't move.

"Son, I can't help you," Patrick cried helplessly. "I – I can't do anything to stop this."

Doug turned his head in the direction of his father's voice. What he saw would have made him cry tears of joy if the circumstances had been different. There was his dad with the tan he had the day he died, standing in the hallway near the door. Doug never thought he'd see his father again – he didn't believe in life after death the way Chris did. When you're dead, you're dead was what he always said. Laying eyes on his father would have made him think he was crazy, he was sure of it, but he would have welcomed the vision. He missed his dad so much.

"Dad." The pain in Doug's face was undeniable.

The Hunter caressed Doug's cheek with the suction cup attached to its left pointer finger, calling Doug's attention back to the beast on top of him. He began to fight it, lifting his legs roughly beneath it, trying to buck it off of him. He punched at it, first in the face, then in the stomach. It didn't block him; it let him wail away until he was tired. The laugh that escaped its lips — Gina's luscious lips that just a half hour before had been kissing Doug in places Chris seldom would — was the most horrible sound Doug had ever heard. He screamed, the sound mingling with hers in a grotesque duet.

The Hunter bore a hole into his chest, burning the skin away. It reached a finger inside the chest cavity and affixed a suction cup to Doug's heart. Before Doug's screams from the burn could die down, it started sucking the heart, pulling it in concert with its natural contractions at first, then accelerating it faster and faster and faster, until the muscle could no longer keep up. Doug's body jerked beneath it, convulsing, his screams long silent. And soon his body stilled as well.

The Hunter glared at Patrick when it was done with Doug, thoroughly satisfied.

"You bastard," Patrick growled.

That drew a smile from the Hunter, one that Patrick could have lived without seeing.

Doug, who entered the afterlife facing the front door of his apartment, his back toward the carnage on his bed, walked toward his father in shock.

"Dad?"

Patrick raced to him and embraced him, enjoying how solid he felt beneath his hands. How human.

"Doug. Doug I'm so sorry."

"What happened?" Doug's eyes strayed toward his body, but found he couldn't look at himself, not with a hole in his chest.

"You died, son. You're dead." Patrick didn't want to say those words, never thought he would have to. They flowed from his mouth like thick syrup from bark.

"But what happened? Gina —." Shame blazed in Doug's cheeks. Did his father know about him and Chris? Did he know what he had done?

"I know all about it, Doug. Maybe we can talk about it some other time, but now isn't it."

Relief spread across Doug's face. "Gina attacked me. She killed me."

"That wasn't Gina. I have to wonder if Gina ever existed."

Doug looked confused.

"That was a Hunter that killed you. Hunter's can shape shift into anything they want to when they leave The Realm. Gina might have just been one of their disguises."

Doug looked back at his body, at the hole in his chest. He put his hand on his new chest and found it open in the same place.

"I know," Patrick said quietly.

"You said The Realm," Doug said, trying to recover. "What is that?"

"It's where we are right now. It's where we'll live for however long eternity is."

Doug's frowned. "Not Heaven or Hell? I fully expected to meet the devil, pitchfork and all after everything I've done."

Patrick couldn't help but laugh. He missed his son's humor. He missed his son.

"Not the Devil. Not God either. But someone else."

Doug shook his head, stealing one last glance at his body as he did it. "I hate being right all the time."

"I wish you had been wrong this time. And if I had been any kind of man you would have been."

Doug looked at his father in surprise. There wasn't anything he could imagine that his father might have done in his life that would make him say such a thing. Then again, he hoped Gabby wouldn't ever know what he had done. A child's ignorance was the best ignorance in the world.

He didn't think Chris would tell her, not with him being... he couldn't bring himself to say the word. It had happened so fast. He was healthy, relatively young. Why did he have to die? He wondered what questions Gabby would have. He wondered what the cause of death would be. How do you explain a hole in the chest? The news was going to hit Gabby hard, he knew. And Chris. He still loved Chris. In fact, had been thinking of trying to start over with her, if she'd let him. But now it was too late.

Doug's thoughts bounced of the walls of his mind, colliding with each other, wrenching free, and starting all over again. He would miss Gabby's prom dress, would miss graduation. He would miss her wedding day – oh God, who would walk her down the aisle? – the birth of her first child. He stole a glance at his father whose head hung low. Patrick was mourning his son's death as much as he was. Doug's eyes watered as he realized his thoughts mirrored what his dad's must have been in his first moments on the other side. He missed Gabby's birth by a matter of months. He had been looking forward to his first grandchild and that joy was stolen from him.

"There is so much I have to tell you," Patrick continued. He felt guilty, ashamed. He didn't know how Doug was going to take the news of his past lives, but he had to tell him. It was his fault that Doug was stuck in The Realm, his fault that Gabby would end up there at the end of her life. He had to own up to what he had done to put them there – all of them. He owed them that much.

CHAPTER FORTY-FIVE

Mileeha enjoyed scaring Milagros – it was easy to do. He supposed any human would react the same as she did given the situation. Even he might have once upon a time. His grandmother used to talk about seeing ghosts all the time, walking in the yard in front of the house and scaring the chickens, and playing in the laundry, like children. Mileeha remembered the fear that welled inside him when she would bolt upright and stare out of the window, seeing something there that he couldn't. He would look at the floor, at her neck with its sagging skin, the wall – he would look at anything to avoid the window and whatever was out there. He could only imagine what his reaction would have been if, on one of those days, the ghost strolling in the yard came up to the window and stuck his head inside.

Milagros' back was as straight as a board, her relaxed posture disappearing as soon as Patrick left the shop. Her lips quivered, Mileeha could see it from where he stood, little pulses, a flit of the tongue over them for a second only to recede behind the teeth. There had been many women, before and after death, but Milagros was one of the most beautiful. She reminded him of a time when he was free, when his only care in the world was getting to the next place fast and the feel of a woman's breast against his chest. There were other things she reminded him of, but he didn't want to think about that then. He wouldn't allow the moment to be ruined by old memories, old ghosts.

"Why are you staring at me that way?" Milagros said, her voice shaking a little, just beneath the surface.

He loved this game.

Milagros fidgeted in her chair in the wake of Mileeha's silence. She was going to die; she knew it. She had finally crossed a line that couldn't be forgiven. And for what? A lost cause? As she watched him stare at her as crudely as a man waiting for his turn with the whore servicing his friend, tears stung her eyes.

"Shouldn't a man look at a woman? Isn't that the way it goes, or have things changed since I last walked the ground you stand on?"

"You aren't a man," Milagros spat, her helplessness transforming into anger. "Not anymore."

Mileeha smiled not unpleasantly as he made his way to her. She cringed away from him, pressing her back into the seat.

"I assure you," Mileeha said, his voice airy and light, "I am."

Milagros fought the urge to turn away. She didn't want to give him the pleasure of knowing he had broken her spirit. Her pride kept telling her that as cold fear covered her skin at the thought of him trying to kiss her.

"You did well," Mileeha said, enjoying the smell of her perfume, the closeness of her body to his. He wanted to touch her but knew that once he started it would be hard to stop. "You did exactly as I asked."

Milagros shook her head. She hadn't tried hard enough to stop Patrick from going. She was afraid. She didn't want to die, especially not over someone who was already dead and was chasing after a lost cause. But no one deserved what he got.

"It's cruel what you've done," she hissed. "What did that man do? What could have possibly done that was so horrible, so evil that you would make him watch his own son die?"Mileeha thought about the question longer than he would have any other. When he answered his voice sounded almost human. "It's not what he's done, but what he will do," Mileeha said. "That man," he said as his finger reached to stroke her leg, his second thoughts forgotten, "will change everything."

Chapter Forty-Six

Patrick told Doug everything by the light of the fire. They sat in the place where he and Dominic had shared camp. Doug protested at first, talking over Patrick and shaking his head violently, as if the words were poisoning him.

"I can't believe it," Doug said when Patrick had finished telling him about his time in The Realm. "Dad, how could you have done all those things?"

"It wasn't me doing them," Patrick responded, knowing how empty the words sounded. They felt just as empty coming out of his mouth. "Not the person you've always known. Doug, you've got to believe me. I've never had an impulse to hurt anyone, never remembered anything about my past lives. I haven't even had a nightmare that was as hellish as what I've done." Patrick's voice wavered and he looked away into the vastness of the forest. "I-I didn't know, Doug. You have to believe that."

Doug believed him. Of course, he did. His father was the nicest guy he knew, and he felt that way even after the pre-adolescent adoration had worn off. Doug didn't think that Patrick, the man he had been before he died, would ever have been able to do the things that the fortuneteller said he did. It was impossible. Why hadn't his good deeds outweighed his bad? Why hadn't there been some sort of clue, some sign as to what needed to be repaid? He didn't want to believe that God could be that cruel.

The account of his father had done filled his mind. Walls covered in blood, people screaming, his father's grinning face standing above them – it scared him to his core. Doug looked away from Patrick until he regained his composure.

"Could she be wrong? I mean, how could she know for sure? This past lives stuff is bullshit – you've never believed in anything like that. How can we be sure she knows what she's talking about?"

"You don't have to believe in them to have them," Patrick said ruefully. "Besides, look around. Does this look like Heaven to you? Or Hell for that matter?"

Doug's emotions were swirling, boiling to the point of bubbling over. He was stuck in this in between place where no one could see them for something that his father did, only it wasn't his father exactly. It was the first incarnation of the man he called Dad, and it happened over 300 years ago. Now Doug was there and Gabby would be too.

"What about Mom?" Doug blurted out as if the words had a life of their own.

"She's not here," Patrick said, a different kind of sadness lacing his words.

"Do you know where she is? She made it to Heaven, right? She can't be in Hell, can she?" Doug rambled on like a child that had too much candy, hardly taking a breath in between.

"I don't know – I think she's in Heaven or Arcadia as they call it."

"Arcadia?" Doug turned away in exasperation. So, not only was there some third world, some purgatory where no amount of repentance could get you out, Heaven wasn't really Heaven anymore. It was Arcadia.

Doug pounded his hand into the cold ground in a forest that, oddly, resembled one near the house where he grew up.

"That's what Mark called it."

Mark. His Dad's brother. Mark sighed, letting the animosity that was building within him out in a flow of hot air.

Doug reclined on the ground that was surprisingly cold, and stared away from his father, away from the place where they sat. He was angry about being in The Realm. It was just as good as Hell to him. He was sad that he was dead. More upset about it than he thought he would be when he was alive and kicking and thinking about ways to take himself out after Chris left. Back then he thought it would be an end to all his troubles, an easy way out. But now, knowing he wouldn't be able to see his family, wouldn't be able to reconcile with Chris, or hug Gabby ever again, he saw things differently. He felt sad for Gabby. She would miss him as much as he would miss her. He would have the luxury of checking in on her life from time to time, though his Dad told him how much he had missed in what seemed like a matter of days (he wondered how much he had already missed just sitting there zoning out), but she wouldn't be able to see him again, except in a coffin. His eyes watered and he let the tears fall.

Patrick sighed heavily, feeling as though he might cry himself. "I know this is hard for you, Doug. It was hard for me too. On my second day here, I was chased by one of those things. I didn't know where I was going; I just knew I had to get off the road and fast. I had to learn by the seat of my pants out here. I met a guy who helped me, but I don't know how much of what he said I can believe anymore."

Patrick shook his head as if deciding to change course.

"I guess what I'm saying is I would do anything in the world to change things for you, son. But I don't think I can. But maybe together we can change things for Gabby."

Patrick watched the flames lick into the sky, remembering that day in front of Doug and Chris's house. Doug and Chris. He hadn't forgotten about that. Seeing Doug lying naked in the arms of another woman bothered him as much as if Joanne had done it to him. He would ask what happened, how he and Chris had gotten to that point, if for nothing more than allowing himself to vent his disappointment. But not then.

"I saw her, you know," Patrick said, the memory of Gabby's angelic little face filling his heart.

"When?" Doug's voice was thick.

"I wanted to see you all. I needed to be sure that you were all right. I found my way to the house and saw you and her playing in the leaves." Doug smiled in spite of the tears wetting his cheek.

"She was so beautiful, so full of life. I couldn't help but stare at her. My granddaughter. And my son."

Patrick patted Doug on the shoulder.

"I have never been prouder of you than I was that day."

Patrick looked into the forest, at the leaves that fell on the tall grass. He imagined his two-and-a-half-year-old granddaughter playing among them, there in The Realm, her hair bouncing around her head, her little hand scooping up leaves tinged with blood. The thought was enough to make him sick.

"I think she saw me. It scared me but I couldn't move. She waved at me with her little finger as you carried her into the house."

Doug's face brightened. "I remember that day. I asked her what she was laughing at. I thought it was the door."

Patrick could hear it creaking in his head as Doug talked about it.

"But she was laughing at you," Doug finished.

"Did she say anything? Did I frighten her?" Patrick's voice was hurried.

"When we got inside, she asked who that man was. I opened the drapes and looked out. There was no one there. I told her so and she giggled again and said the man was nice. I laughed it off and then she laughed and pretty soon we forgot all about it. She was frightened at all, Dad. She was tickled pink about it."

Patrick smiled, his fears stilled. Gabby saw him. She really saw him. He wondered what he must have looked like to her, if she recognized him. He wanted to ask but thought better about it. Sometimes the fantasy was better than the truth.

"God, that must have been twelve, thirteen years ago," Doug surmised.

"For me it was only last week."

Doug stared at Patrick who kept looking forward, off in the distance. More than ten years floated by in a week's time. He couldn't help wondering how long he'd been there, how long he'd been dead. Had Gabby graduated fro high school already? College? Had Chris remarried? He wanted to ask but he didn't think his father would know any better than he did.

"This can't be happening," Doug said, his emotions taking over again. "This can't be true." It all seemed surreal, that place, his death. It was like a horrible nightmare.

Patrick touched Doug's arm and was happy to find that he didn't pull away. "I'm sorry, son. I really am, but I have to believe we can do something about this."

Doug looked at Patrick through teary eyes. "What are you talking about? I thought you said we couldn't get out of The Realm. Ever. God's punishment and all."

"I know that's what I said, but I can't believe it's true, not completely. I was a man of the cloth. God showed favor on me all those times. I blew it but he didn't send me to Hell. He sent me here, to this limbo-like place. Why?"

The question hung in the air.

"That has to mean something," Patrick finished.

Doug brightened suddenly, his face transforming from the deep-lined scowl it was before to that of a man who saw promise. Patrick was afraid to hear what he would say next, afraid that he would have to let his son down again. "Maybe he hasn't shut the door all the way yet," Doug said hopefully. "Maybe there's still a chance we can get out of here."

Patrick felt horrible. It was too soon to bombard Doug with all the ideas that had been floating around his mind since he'd gotten there. Doug needed to get acclimated to The Realm in his way. Giving him false hope wouldn't do anything but hurt him. But it was too late now. He had to keep going.

"I don't know if we can get out, son," Patrick said as gently as he could. He hoped the tone was conciliatory and not condescending. "I think it's too late for us because… because we're already dead."

The sadness etched on Doug's face made Patrick want to die all over again and never wake up.

"But it might not be too late for Gabby. Or anyone else."

Doug looked at Patrick, who was looking at some unseen thing in the distance, over the hilltop, a new fire lighting in his eyes.

CHAPTER FORTY-SEVEN

Tara watched as Patrick and Doug talked. She couldn't hear him from where she hid, but she didn't need to. She could tell what was going on by the looks on their faces, their postures, their auras. They were planning. Plotting. Scheming.

Tara had plans after all, ones she had been working on since she found herself in The Realm all those years ago. She started as soon as she realized who had put her there.

Tara watched them, father and son damned to the same fate, as they planned, plotted and schemed and smiled as the breeze cooled her cheeks.

CHAPTER FORTY-EIGHT

Sebastian saw a figure on the hilltop closest to where the rest of The Watchers were camped. He knew better than to follow her, to join her when she hadn't asked for company. She was focused and he didn't want to feel her wrath when interrupted.

Her intensity scared him. It was more than just trailing a Hunter and killing him for food. More than just trying to find a hole in The Realm so they could get out. For Tara there was something else just beneath the surface. The only thing that seemed to matter was following the new guy. Why, he didn't exactly know.

Sebastian had no delusions about where he stood with her. Theirs was a relationship of convenience. Her heart was elsewhere. Sebastian thought it might be with Patrick, but that didn't feel totally right to him. Patrick had something to do with it, but he didn't know what. Every time he tried to talk to Tara about it, she would leave, would go off on one of her walks, walks that could last days. He waited for her to come back, never moving camp. He kept The Watchers in line, when she was gone even though they didn't want to be. They were restless. They felt vulnerable to the Hunters. He was running out of reasons to stay. He was also running out of answers as to why Tara was tracking Patrick.

Aadi asked him just that day what they were doing. "I thought the plan was to find a way out of here. We can't do that just sitting around here."

"I know," Sebastian had said, dismayed that it had been Aadi that had come to him. If Aadi, the quietest one of the bunch, had concerns, they all did. "But we can't leave until Tara comes back."

"What is she doing? Why is she tracking this guy so closely?" Sebastian didn't answer.

"It's not safe to stay in one place so long, Sebastian, you know that. The Hunters have probably sniffed us out already and are just waiting to get hungry."

"I understand how you feel Aadi," Sebastian said wearily, "but we can't leave without Tara. She'll be back soon. I think her mission is almost done."

Aadi said nothing more. He went back to his bunk and turned away from where Sebastian stood. He didn't talk with anyone about their conversation, and wouldn't – Aadi never felt the need to commiserate. For the first time since knowing him, Sebastian was thankful for that.

Aadi's words told him what everyone was thinking — they wanted to move on and to find another camp. They want to cover more ground and recruit more Watchers. They wanted to go on living as best they could until they found a way out of The Realm. So did he.

Sebastian watched Tara, her body still and unmoving, as she sat on the hilltop, illuminated only by the little bit of moon left in the midnight sky. And waited.

CHAPTER FORTY-NINE

Patrick and Doug awoke early the next morning. Doug felt fresh, more so than he ever felt upon waking. It was obscene feeling good, considering the hole that gaped open in his chest (he tried to convince himself that he wasn't really feeling the air blowing through the hole, but so far it wasn't working). He thought about all the things he would miss about being alive. And there were a lot of them.

Patrick stretched as he stood though he didn't really need to. His back hadn't given him any trouble since he landed in The Realm. He woke up feeling like could run ten miles before opening his eyes. He relished the thought — he and Doug were going to need their strength. It may not save their hides, but at least it'll help them fight a little longer. Patrick wanted to fight. He owed it to Doug.

Without a word they started out, abandoning the ground on which they spent the night and shared their plan. They walked the forest up the incline that led to the road and headed west, in the direction of Mileeha's house.

CHAPTER FIFTY

Tara moved along the hilltop until she was sure. When Patrick and Doug rounded the bend in the path, going back the way Patrick had come his second day in The Realm, she knew. An unexpected uneasiness set in as she watched them, their backs growing further and further away with every step. She turned into the dense forest, making her way down to the flat land where The Watchers waited.

It was time.

Chapter Fifty-One

Sebastian saw her coming before anyone else did. He wanted to be elated; he wanted to be happy to see her again. But he wasn't. Instead, his heart was filled with dread. The look on her face confirmed everything he feared.

"They're going," Tara said breathlessly. "They're really going to do it."

Sebastian embraced her and winced when she didn't reciprocate.

"Did you hear me?" she said, her voice more forceful. "They're going. Now."

"What are you talking about, Tara? What have you been doing for the past couple of days?"

Sebastian asked the question knowing the answer already; he'd been trailing her as much as she had been trailing Patrick. He needed to hear her say it, needed to know what her obsession with Patrick was, for once and for all. He was tired of coming up with conclusions on his own. He wanted to hear the truth from her own mouth.

Tara ignored his question and moved to wake the rest of the group. Aadi was the only one who had been sleeping; he had slept through his own murder much the same way. Lydjauk had been listening to their conversation. He had been doing something else also. He probed Tara's mind to find out what she was so wound up about. The answer made his tentacles recoil in fear.

"He's doing it," Tara said to The Watchers, her own little band of brothers. She let her eyes fall on each of them, sizing them up. "Patrick and his son Doug are actually going to do it."

"Do what, Tara?" Sebastian asked. "And why should any of us care what your lover does?"

Tara turned to him in surprise. She heard the pain in his voice and it struck her as odd. Sure, Sebastian seemed interested in her, but she had made it clear that what was between them was purely physical. For him, though, it was more than that.

"My lover? You think Patrick is my lover?"

Tara laughed in spite of herself. She didn't want to humiliate him, but she couldn't help it. She couldn't bring herself to tell him the truth then; it would have been cruel. He would figure it out on his own before too much time had passed, she thought. And by then, it might not matter anymore.

"Patrick is not my lover. He was not my lover when we were alive either, in any life, though I do believe we have crossed paths before." She searched Sebastian's face for a reaction and found relief loosening his brown and softening his eyes. It broke her heart.

"Patrick and his son are going to the house where Mileeha dwells. They are planning to kill him."

"You're shittin' me," Kincaid said, a cynical laugh tickling the back of his throat. "They haven't been here, but a minute and they think they can kill Mileeha?"

"They'll die trying," Qiao added, shaking his head.

"Now that's the smartest thing I've heard you say yet," Kincaid said, punching Qiao in the arm.

"I wouldn't be so sure," Lydjauk said.

"What are you talking about?" Kincaid's voice rose a notch. "You can't seriously think those two puppies could have a chance against Mileeha and The Hunters. They'd be eaten a live."

"They haven't been yet," Aadi said quietly. "There must be a reason for that."

"They've been lucky, that's all there is to it," Kincaid surmised. "Let them sleep out on the road one night. I bet you a Hunter'll come around quiet-like and tear them to pieces before they ever knew what hit 'em. Mileeha's playing with them is all. He's playing with all of us."

"Why are you telling us this?" Sebastian asked, more afraid than he had been before.

"Because I want all of you," she said, extending her arm in a sweeping gesture, "to come with me. I want us to help them."

Silence.

Tara's smile faded as she looked into the faces of the ones she had chosen to hunt the Hunters. She looked into each of their eyes and didn't like what she saw.

"This is what we've all been working toward. What did you think we were doing out here? Killing Hunters for sport?" Her voice teetered on shrill.

"You can't be serious Tara," Sebastian started and was cut off by a look that could have killed.

"I assure you I am," Tara hissed.

"Why should we help them? They're walking into a minefield and we should be smart enough to hang behind. We know what they're up against. Kincaid's eyes were wide and his mouth was twisted in an amused grin. "It's suicide."

Tara looked at all of them, one by one, and saw the same sentiment. She shook her head and took a step away, wanting to leave their presence as though their skepticism was contagious.

"Suicide," she mumbled and then laughed loudly. "You speak as if we have lives to lose. How much worse could it be to die at Mileeha's hands? Surely it can't be any worse than dying the first time, could it? And I know it can't be worse than being on guard every waking moment. Why haven't we just let the Hunters get us? Who knows? It could be the way to Hell."

"They'd eat us before we even got close," Sebastian said in a calm voice. "Either that or turn us into one of them. Whatever else comes, I don't want to be a Hunter."

"Maybe they will," Tara said sarcastically, "but maybe they won't. Maybe Patrick and Doug can distract them in front and we can take them from behind."

"You don't mind sacrificing them?" Sebastian asked, his voice getting louder with every word. He was starting to see Tara for what she was. She trailed Patrick since the moment he entered The Realm, fed them all a line about how he could be an excellent recruit for the Watchers, and they bought it. In reality he was nothing to her; she didn't care if he lived or died. He was nothing more than bait.

Tara looked at him with eyes that were as icy as first snow. The coldness was almost palpable. But there was something else lingering there as well, something he didn't quite understand… or wouldn't allow himself to.

"I want to get Mileeha." Her voice was as low as a growl.

"Why?" Qiao asked seemingly from out of nowhere. "Why do you want Mileeha so bad? He's nothing more than Mal's second. He does whatever Mal wants him to do. Mileeha isn't the one who brought us all to The Realm. Mal did."

Lydjauk stared at Qiao, admiring him for his guts. He didn't recoil when Tara shot him a look after his first question; he kept pressing. It looked back at Tara, interested in her answer.

Tara's neck felt warm. She didn't know if she should tell them everything. Would it make them come with her? Probably not. Would anything? She didn't know. Keeping the truth to herself would be better than spilling it for all of them to see, she decided quickly. The look in Sebastian's eyes convinced her of that.

"Mal is too big," Tara started, not knowing exactly where her lie would take her. She had been a good liar in life. She only hoped the trait had stuck with her. "Mileeha is nothing if separated from him. Yes, he has powers beyond anything we have, but I think, if we get him alone, if we surprise him, he'll be defenseless."

Tara waited for more skepticism, more questions about her so-called plan, but got none. The blank stares on their faces made her form more empty words to speak.

"He'll be alone, except for a few Hunters, but they are easy to fool, we already know that." The Watchers had been running circles around The Hunters for what seemed like decades. They were easily confused, easily distracted. The key was traveling in pairs, threes if possible. And running. Lots and lots of running.

"Mal will be off somewhere else," Tara continued, hoping they recalled what she had taught them at the very beginning. Even then she was planting the seed of retribution against Mileeha. She told them that though Mal shared the house with Mileeha, he was rarely there. No one knew what Mal did although she thought he watched the lives of the marked like a person watching a movie, but he had put Mileeha in a position of authority for one reason only: he had more pressing issues to deal with. Tara hoped they remembered her words, hoped they had believed them.

"Where? Having tea with the Devil?"

"He'll be gone. You know it as much as I do," Tara continued, looking each of them in the eye.

"We'll watch until Patrick and Doug enter the house. Mileeha will sense them long before they walk through the door. He will have planned his attack by the time they take their first step inside. It's when he begins to execute his plan, when he takes them by the neck and lifts them from the floor, that we come in. And then we kill him. We cut his head off and feed his body to The Hunters. Without the head they won't know who they're eating – they're brainless creatures. It'll just be meat to them."

That part was true. Tara relished the idea of ripping Mileeha's head from his neck and feeding his body to the beasts he created. The look of surprise and of fear frozen on his face was one she would never forget. And she would do it; she knew she would. After a kiss.

"What if Mileeha doesn't go after them? What if he senses our presence and turns to find us standing there with meager weapons; a woman, three men, and an alien with nothing more to arm them than makeshift spears and stones. What then?" Sebastian challenged her because he saw right through her elaborate plan. He saw through her. The newfound clarity was like a black veil being lifted from a mother's face (much like the veil he was sure his mother had worn at his funeral all those years ago). The Realm seemed clearer to him. Tara's secret stood out like a drop of blood on a white shirt.

Tara cast a measured glance at Sebastian and suddenly felt as naked as the day she was reborn in The Realm.

"I will keep his attention," she said, her voice low, as if the answer was only intended for the questioner. "I'll find some way."

Sebastian didn't press, though he could have. She had run out of line and was teetering on the edge of exposing herself for the manipulator she had been. It might have already been too late, Sebastian though as he looked at his partners. Their faces registered the confusion they felt. Their days of following her were over.

Tara saw the same coldness in their faces, but she saw something else too: anger. She took a step backward, and then another before turning on her heel and walking back in the direction she came.

"I won't ask you again," she called over her shoulder.

The Watchers stood still, watching her leave.

Tara pressed on, through the woods and around countless bends, leaving The Watchers behind. She didn't give them the satisfaction of a backwards glance.

CHAPTER FIFTY-TWO

Patrick and Doug could see the house. It was only a stone's throw away. They buried themselves in the brush and peered out at it.

"I don't think anyone saw us," Doug said, whispering almost inaudibly.

Patrick cast a glance over his should at the trees, at the thick expanse of land behind them. He knew they'd been spotted. He was banking on it.

The house looked more like a shack up close than it had in the distance. The wood seemed to be rotting away. The door was plain – it was nothing more than a board with a knob midway between on the right side. No lock. Patrick guessed Mileeha and Mal didn't have a need for locks—who in their right mind would bother them? He would. He and Doug. It was their only chance.

A couple of Hunters milled around aimlessly in the tall grass behind the house. They were like voodoo zombies awaiting a command from the one that controlled their souls. Patrick was no longer afraid of them. If he was supposed to become a meal for one of them, it would have happened already. There was something else he was supposed to do, something he was being preserved for. That it could be the very mission he and his son had embarked on floated around in his mind like a whisper.

Patrick might not have been afraid of the Hunters, but Doug was. He had never seen anything as heinous in his life… except for the moment he died. He jerked backwards when he saw one looking in their direction.

"Oh God! It's those things! They see us. We gotta get outta here!"

Doug rose to run and Patrick grabbed his arm.

"What the hell are you doing? They'll maul us!"

"It's all right," Patrick said in a calm yet amused voice. "They're not going to hurt us."

Doug looked at his father in confusion. He sat down on the grass next to him, waiting for an explanation.

"They know we're here, you're right. But they aren't going to do anything to us."

"How can you know that?" Doug's voice was on the edge of hysteria.

Patrick turned to face his son. "Doug, I've been chased by a couple of these things. I've kept my camp unhidden, not out of cockiness, but out of ignorance. And they've never touched me. Even the ones that chased me. They could have easily caught me, but they gave chase long enough for me to think I was a goner, and then they backed off."

Patrick looked back at the house before continuing. "It's like they know they can't touch me. It's like I'm not supposed to be a meal."

"That doesn't scare you?" Doug was calming down a little. That his father was safe from the Hunters didn't mean he was – a fact that crushed him like a weight.

Patrick looked into the woods again. "What can they do to us, I mean really, Doug? If they eat us and we stay dead, they're putting us out of our misery. If they send us to Hell, I can't imagine it'd be much worse than this. I think Heaven is out of the question. No brother of Satan's would have a deal with God."

"They could make us Hunters or Parasics, or whatever you called them. That's what you said happened to Dominic. I couldn't be one of those things, chasing people down and... and eating them. It's disgusting. One of those people I'd eat might end up being Gabby."

Doug stopped speaking after saying his daughter's name. Gabby would be terrified in The Realm. She never liked the woods. Only the leaves. Even at sixteen, she still liked to jump in the raked leaves and make a mess of them again. The trees, the sounds, the absolute darkness when night fell, would terrify her. She didn't deserve a place like that, where there seemed to be nothing but endless trees and vast forest. She wouldn't have to be sent to Hell, she would already be there.

"They could do that Doug, you're right. But I have to hope that the Parasics are as dead as our bodies are and that they don't know what they're doing. To me it's worth the risk to try and save Gabby and the rest of our line, but if you don't want to do this, you don't have to. Those Hunters seem to know not to touch me, but I can't say they've been told the same about you."

Doug smiled inadvertently. It was uncanny how he and his father could be thinking the same thing a couple of second apart. They always laughed it off, but there was something to it, he saw now. There was something to everything it seemed.

"No," Doug said, rising up on his haunches, "I'm in. Let's go."

Doug took a hesitant first step and a surer second one. Patrick cast one last glance over his shoulder before following.

Chapter Fifty-Three

Mileeha saw Tara trailing behind Patrick and Doug as easily as if her were watching the scene through a looking glass. She skulked along, trying to stay hidden, but even the older man could sense her. He smiled; she had never been any good at playing hide and seek.

The time had finally come. He knew the plan; he had heard it in her disjointed thoughts before she convinced herself of them. She knew Mal wasn't there. Patrick and Doug would come through the front because there were Hunters around back— even though Patrick was sure they wouldn't touch him, he didn't want to run the risk of losing his son. Not again. He didn't think he could handle seeing him die a second time. There was another reason, though it was buried deep inside his mind: he didn't want to recognize one of them as Dominic.

So predictable.

The one who Patrick had known as Dominic was already dead. He had been killed by Mileeha's own hand and fed to the rest of his

Hunters. He served no other purpose outside of his work with Patrick. He was no longer needed.

Tara thought Patrick and Doug would distract him when they came in the front door. He could have dispatched with them easily, without more than a second's work, but he would let himself be taken unawares. He would let Tara pull up the rear and ambush him. Once she was inside the house Patrick and Doug would be of no use to him. He would let the Hunters do as they would with them, giving only one directive: after they were done playing with their new toys, they were to destroy them.

Then he would have Tara to himself.

Mileeha laid back in the old recliner he placed in the house, a remnant from one of his past lives, and waited.

CHAPTER FIFTY-FOUR

Sebastian watched Tara until she was gone. He shouldn't have let her go. If she was hell-bent on taking Mileeha down, she couldn't do it alone. But why did she want him so badly? Why was killing him such a big deal to her?

He knew the answer. He just didn't want to believe it.

Mileeha was the shadow over them, the one link to her lives that she couldn't shake. He was her love, the one she told him about. He was the man that condemned her.

She hated him; he knew she did. She wanted to make him pay for landing her in The Realm; she wanted him to suffer. Tara never let on that the one she was after, the one she would kill as soon as she found him, was Mileeha.

Mileeha. Of all the people in The Realm to have a vendetta against, Tara had to have one against the right-hand man of Mal. The only thing worse was a vendetta against Mal himself.

As much as Tara hated Mileeha, Sebastian thought she still loved him as strongly, if not more. She was too driven, too determined for hate to be the only force behind her. His stomach cramped, almost doubling him over.

Tara had made a fool of him. Sebastian felt like everyone was staring at him after she left. She left and would probably never be back, leaving him to pick up the pieces.

But he loved her. God, he loved her.

"And so do I," a voice said behind him. Sebastian turned to see Lydjauk standing with him, its eyes trained on the same spot Sebastian's had been.

"I didn't know I had those kinds of emotions, didn't think it was possible," Lydjauk continued, "But I do. It's not the same as you— I have no interest in copulating with her— but I do love her."

Sebastian nodded and turned back to the path empty now in Tara's wake.

"She'll die if she goes against Mileeha alone."

"We'll all die if we help her," Sebastian said flatly.

"We're dead already. What could be worse?"

Sebastian seemed to think about that for a while. His answer came suddenly, his voice on the edge of alarm. "We could be one of those." Sebastian pointed at a Hunter skulking in the distance. He started to move backward, further into the camp. He was about to warn the others, to tell them to hide, when Lydjauk said, "Sebastian, haven't you wondered how we're able to capture the Hunters? Those hulking, beastly things with senses as keen as mine, if not better, how are we able to trap them and kill them?"

Sebastian started to speak, but found he had nothing to say.

"Why haven't they hunted us down and killed us? W go off on our own all the time, certainly Tara does. Why have there never been attacks on us?"

"There's a reason, Sebastian," Lydjauk said, "There's a reason for everything."

The two stood looking at the path Tara had used to go to Mileeha. Without speaking, Lydjauk implanted one thought in Sebastian's mind: "Maybe we can help Tara after all. Maybe we're meant to."

CHAPTER FIFTY-FIVE

Patrick and Doug had moved closer to the front door of the house and were hunkered down behind a patch of overgrown bushes. Patrick couldn't help feeling the way he felt the first time he saw the rickety place, couldn't shake how much it reminded him of those houses on the way up to Skyline Drive. The atmosphere made Patrick feel like he was back home, like he might still be alive. It was enough to slow him down. Enough to make him relish it a bit longer.

It was enough to make him think of Joanne again.

"What are we waiting on? Let's get this over with," Doug said impatiently.

"Just a minute more." Patrick was looking at the brush at the back of the house. He saw her, the girl that had been trailing he and Doug. The girl who watched him from afar every once in a while. He never had the chance to talk to her, didn't think she'd stick around if he approached her anyway. He knew she wasn't trouble; she could have killed him easily several times. Patrick knew she would be there that day, just as he knew she had been there the night before, watching him and Doug while they talked. She was supposed to be there. They fit into her plan as well as she fit into theirs.

Patrick wondered if she knew she was being watched. He wondered if she cared.

He and Doug would enter the house through the front door and she would follow from around back—her immunity to the Hunters perplexed him but there was no time to think about what it meant. This is what she had always wanted, what she had known he was going to do. Why else would she be there?

When he was ready, Patrick tapped Doug. Doug's nerves were wired tight; he nearly jumped out of his skin at his father's hand touch.

"You ready?"

"Yeah," Doug breathed.

"Let's do it."

CHAPTER FIFTY-SIX

The door creaked loudly as Patrick and Doug opened it. For a moment Patrick thought the game was over. But nothing happened. The room was empty and there were no sounds coming from upstairs or the back room.

The air was laced with the smell of sweet potato pie. The room was warm and cozy. Patrick knew the place. It hadn't looked familiar to him on the outside, though something about it made him feel good, made him feel like he was home. It was his grandmother's house, a place he hadn't been since he was seven years old.

"How?" Patrick muttered, vocalizing the thought. He walked into the main room, which served as living room and dining room without hiding — somehow, he knew there was no need for that anymore. In the corner sat his chair, the one that his grandfather had fashioned out of wood slats and nails. A fire was burning in the fireplace — his grandmother loved a warm fire after the day was done. A patchwork quilt was draped over the back of the sofa, just as it had been the last time he was in the house.

It had to be a figment of his imagination, he kept telling himself, but he couldn't make his eyes believe it. The house he and Doug were in was his grandmother's house, no question about it. It was the place in his childhood that meant the most to him. He hadn't realized how much until right then.

"Grandma?" Patrick called, knowing she would come through the door from the kitchen at the sound of his voice. She was always as happy as he was to see her. And she was baking that pie just for him; he knew it. "Grandma, I'm here!"

Doug elbowed Patrick in the ribs hard enough to get a reaction.

"What are you doing?" Patrick said.

"What are you doing? You're gonna get us caught!"

"This is my grandma's house. We're in her house. I don't know how this can be, but we're here."

Doug's eyes clouded over. Patrick couldn't read the expression in them. "Dad, this isn't your grandmother's house. This is *your* house."

Patrick looked around again, still seeing the walls of his grandmother's house, still seeing the holey run and the old furniture. He could still smell the pie too. And he couldn't shake the feeling that she could come from the kitchen at any minute and plant a big kiss on his cheek. She would hug him hard, squeezing him until he felt like he couldn't breath. And he would love it, every minute of it. He had wanted a hug from his grandmother since the day he found out she died. Just one more hug. One more kiss. One more pie. Patrick started to shake his head when Doug spoke,

"The TV is catty-corned to the window and your chair is right across from it. You move it there every night after Mom moves it back to where it's supposed to go. She says your messing up the room, that it looks junky when you move the chair there. And besides, you're not supposed to sit so close to the television anyway."

"One of my comic books is open on the sofa. I can hear the dishwasher running in the background and the show you're watching. *Cheers*. I'll never forget the music to that show. *'Sometimes you wanna go where everybody knows your name -.* '"

"How can that be?" Patrick cut in. "How can we be standing in the same room and see two different places all together?"

"It can be whatever you want it to be," a voice said from behind them, in front of them, all around them at once. "All you have to do is think it."

CHAPTER FIFTY-SEVEN

Mal didn't look the way they expected him to.

Patrick had always imagined he'd be eight feet tall and as wide as a truck. He would have massive arms and huge thighs. He would wear an outfit much like Caesar's in a chariot race, his bare legs glistening in the light as though oiled. His head would be mammoth sitting on top of a wide, thick neck. Patrick hadn't gone as far as to determine what his face might look like – he didn't think he could. *To seek the face of evil is like dying ten times over.* He didn't know where he'd heard the phrase, but it resonated, even in death.

But now, standing in front of the man, the beast that created this world, Patrick stared unabashed.

Mal looked like a regular guy. He was a large, muscular man, but not obscenely so – everything was proportioned and normal looking. He was tallish but no more than 6'5". He wore clothes, though from what time period, Patrick wasn't sure.

"Not what you expected?" Mal asked in a pleasant baritone. "Those that see me always have the same reaction. Then again, there aren't many that see me at all." Patrick was stunned. He didn't understand why he wasn't surprised to see Mal there and not Mileeha. He didn't understand how he knew who was before him, but he did. Patrick knew things about The Realm without being told – he was more connected to the place than he wanted to acknowledge.

"I didn't expect it to be you," Patrick offered.

Mal smiled congenially, "There's that."

Mal was sitting in a chair across from where they stood. The room had changed while they studied him, melting, morphing into some place else, somewhere neither of them had ever been, without them even noticing. Patrick's grandmother's house, with its crackling fire and its old, worn furniture, was gone. As he looked around at the burnt orange painted walls and art deco furniture, he wondered if it had ever been there at all.

"This is one of my favorite rooms. It's in the house of a wealthy clothing designer in California. In his house, it overlooks the hills where smaller houses are lined up in a row, one right next to the other. Since neither of you has ever been there, I decided to use it for our first meeting."

His conversational tone threw Doug off. He expected to be attacked, to be disintegrated by fire, to have his head twisted off his neck. Instead Mal, the brother of Satan, the ruler of The Realm, was talking to them as if he had invited them into his home for drinks.

Mal shifted his legs, folding one over the other in an incredibly human gesture. Was he human? Doug had so many questions.

"We have a proposition for you," Patrick said, finding his tongue.

"I know all about what you want to do, there's no need for you to say it," Mal said, sounding bored. Patrick was surprised, but not totally. He would have to remember it though, and would have to get Doug to do the same. "I think it's a good idea."

"What?" Doug blurted out before he could stop himself. Doug was surprised to still be alive, to still be standing on his own feet. Hearing Mal's agreement was more than he could have ever imagined.

"Right now, things are happening that you don't know about. Your father knows a little, but not as much as he thinks. Your proposition comes right on time. You will be filling an empty slot."

"But the slot isn't empty," Patrick added, feeling strangely comfortable talking to the being who ticked his name off the Book of the Condemned and sent Hunters for him. "Mileeha still lives."

"You want him dead?" Mal asked incredulously. With a sardonic chuckle, Mal said, "Abbadon would have welcomed you with open arms."

"I don't see how we could be your right-hand men with Mileeha still alive. Surely, he would want his post back. He could pose a problem."

Mal nodded as though mulling the idea over. "He will be dead before the end of this day anyway, but I am happy to know that you considered it necessary. Strength is a quality that will serve you well in this job. Judgment. A cool head. Mileeha is exhibiting none of these and that is why his time is finished."

Patrick nodded. He knew Doug was confused. This wasn't the plan at all. But somehow Patrick knew it was what was supposed to happen all along. He hoped Doug could hold his tongue and go with it. They needed to chummy up with Mal, to get him to think they bought into it all. Only then would they be in position to help Gabby. He didn't know if that meant asking Mal to grant a reprieve or protecting her behind his back. They would have time to figure that out once this part of it was over.

If it's over, a little voice in the back of his mind chimed. *If it's over.*

Concern tickled the back of his throat like a cough, but he swallowed it back. He and Doug needed to be in Mileeha's position.

"Let me get this straight," Doug said, "You're gonna let us be second in command just because we had the balls to waltz in and ask? You'd kill your son to move us, two wet behind the ears strangers, in place?"

"My son?" Mal's laugh reminded Patrick of his grandfathers: rich and full. "Who told you Mileeha was my son?"

Doug looked at Patrick and Patrick motioned toward the window. In the second's time he had to look out of the window, he glimpsed five figures creeping along the incline of the land leading towards the house. They were going toward the back door.

"That's what they told me out there."

"Mileeha is no more my son than I am the brother of the Devil."

Patrick's raised his eyebrows.

"You can't believe everything you hear," Mal said as he tried to recover. "I am not human, if you're wondering. I can appear as whatever present company is comfortable with. I am not a brother of Lucifer's, though on a good day I might call him friend. I am not a God. I am not a demon. I just am. I complete the trinity of the afterlife. Without me and without The Realm, it would all fall apart. The same with Arcadia and Abbadon; each part depends upon the others.

"Mileeha," Mal continued, "is just an evil bastard who killed with relish in all of his lives. He knew what he had done in his past; he had the gift of clairvoyance throughout all of his lives. But he didn't change. He didn't want to change. He started killing because his father did in one life, because his sister did in another. Someone else always brought him along, showed him the ropes, made him a killer. That's why he's here and not in Hell. He didn't choose to kill on his own. He got a taste for it after someone showed him how and he kept doing it. His sister and father are in Hell, as are the other ones that showed him the ropes. But he went sent to my doorstep.

"He came in as bold as you two did, with a plan in mind too," Mal continued, seeming to enjoy giving the history lesson. "He told me that he wasn't going to run for eternity; he would just let one of them tear him up. He was dead already, he said, so what was the difference?

Patrick remembered Doug saying those same words hours before and wondered if that might be some sort of omen.

"He talked a good game. I knew he was capable of ruthlessness; I watched his lives very carefully. So, I took a chance. I've been happy with him up until now. Now he's letting his heart overrule his mind."

Mal cut his eyes at the door to what would have been Patrick's grandmother's kitchen before continuing, "It's time to move on."

"What do you see in us that makes you think we are right for the job?" Doug asked. Patrick hoped the question didn't push Mal to the edge. They were on a roll. They were getting what they wanted without a fuss. Maybe they should just count their blessings.

Mal found the question clever, but not intentionally so. Doug was a bit of a hotrod; he wanted to know everything right then and there. He took what he wanted from it, which was never much, and moved on to the next pressing topic. He was controllable. Mal was sure Patrick would see to it that Doug kept in line. But the question was a good one. Mal didn't want to say too much, didn't want to show them how integral the priest was to his plans. Mal smiled as he answered, looking at Patrick all the while. "Neither of you wants to see the other die again."

CHAPTER FIFTY-EIGHT

Sebastian and the rest of the Watchers skulked along the trees, watching surveilled the house. Patrick and Doug had already gone in and they could see Tara waiting by what looked like an old well for her chance to slip by the Hunters.

"Why doesn't she just go?" Kincaid whispered harshly. He was still pissed about having to come along but staying in the woods of The Realm by himself wasn't much of an option. He spent two weeks out there by himself when he woke up from death, and that was plenty.

"She's afraid. Wouldn't you be?" Aadi's calm voice brought Kincaid's own down a notch.

"If this is what I wanted, to get in there and take care of Mileeha, then no. She's been setting this whole thing up since I've been here."

Aadi shook his head and said, "If the love of your life was inside, no matter how much you thought you hated her, how much you wanted to kill her, you would hesitate too."

Sebastian shot a look at Aadi then lowered his eyes.

Kincaid mumbled something under his breath. No one but Lydjauk heard him and it wished it hadn't. It didn't know if it was just Kincaid's anger over the situation or his hateful spirit. Under his breath, Kincaid said, "I hope the Hunters tear her apart before she can even reach the door."

CHAPTER FIFTY-NINE

Tara froze. She was there and ready to go in. She wanted to lodge her spear into the base of Mileeha's spine while she glared into his eyes. But there was something else she wanted. Something she wouldn't allow herself to think about before, wouldn't let herself nurture. But now, sitting outside of the place where he slept, she couldn't deny it.

She wanted him.

All of her anger, all of her desire to avenger her death was melting away by the well near his house. How could she be so stupid? So lovestruck? He condemned her to The Realm as much as he had been. She hated him for introducing her to killing, but in the same breath she missed the feeling. It was exhilarating, running someone down and slicing their throats, driving really fast and letting her hair blow in the wind. She missed it, even though it sickened her to think of how many people she killed. She missed him.

Tara jarred herself awake and peered around the corner of the well. There were Hunters near the door, but they weren't so close that they could snatch her as she went inside. She would be four paces in front of them, even with their long legs and quickness. She had a chance.

Tara ran, crouched over, her head swiveling on her neck as she checked for Hunters. She opened the door and slipped inside in one fluid motion. At the same time The Watchers left the safety of the trees and ran toward the house. Patrick and Doug stood before Mal in the front room of the house watching them as they came. Mal saw them in Patrick's eyes, never having to turn his head.

Chapter Sixty

Mileeha saw Tara enter the kitchen through the darkness that shrouded the room. His heart leapt, as he knew it would. She was the one, in every life, that he could never resist.

Tara found the light switch and turned it on. The light illuminated a kitchen from her youth. The kitchen in her uncle's house. She looked around in awe. Pots hung from a makeshift rack above the stove, the wood cabinets gleamed white from a fresh painting. She smelled sweet molasses and homemade jam from her uncle's preserves stash. She used to love to come downstairs in the morning and have biscuits with his strawberry preserves.

The table sat where it always had: right in the middle of the floor. He used to bump in to it all the time when he was cooking – it was far too big for the tiny room. One of the legs had broken off and been repaired at least five times, the façade was scratched like someone took a knife to it. But he loved it. He wouldn't push it against the wall, wouldn't exchange it for a newer, smaller one. That was the way her uncle was. Old was better than new. Old was vintage whereas new was just... new. She hadn't seen him in at least thirty years.

Tara stepped into the room, breathing in the sweet smell. It was like she was there. She almost expected to see her uncle coming through the door from the living room, hollering

"I thought you'd like it."

Tara recoiled, taking a step backwards and banging into the door behind her. Mileeha was sitting in a chair on the far side of the kitchen table. He was smiling at her.

She raised her spear.

"What? No smile for me? After everything I did? Making the kitchen your uncle used to have?"

Tara stared at him in disbelief.

"You came all this way and you can't even give me a smile?"

He was eating away at the thin veneer of strength she had, and he knew it. Tara fidgeted, shifting from foot to foot.

"How did you do this?" she asked in spite of herself. She told herself not to care, not to listen. Her only reason for being there was to kill him, not to make nice.

"I can do this and more. I can make any room you want. Any landscape you want. All you have to do is tell me."

His silky voice was getting to her. She knew he was turning on the charm, trying to soften her up, but she couldn't help the way she felt. Tara struggled against her emotions, trying to keep her love down and hold on to her anger. She palmed the grip on the spear and tried to regain her composure.

"This is your fault!" she started. "It's your fault I'm here, you bastard!"

Mileeha managed to look stricken. "If I recall, you enjoyed it. Every time." Tara's stare was empty. "I would never have made you do anything you didn't want to do," Mileeha said, his voice dropping to a breathy whisper. "I loved you."

Tara broke. Her animosity flew out of the window. Her love for him, the feel of his arms around her, the touch of his lips, all of it came rushing back. She tried to hold the spear up with the point facing him, but her arm was too heavy.

"I wouldn't be here if it wasn't for you. I didn't want to kill anyone. I never did anything to anyone before you came along and ruined my life."

Mileeha laughed. It was a rich and inviting sound. "I ruined your life. Tara, you would have been killing on your own if I hadn't come along. I don't believe in the idea that someone can make you do something. If you didn't want to kill, you wouldn't have."

"I would have lost you," Tara said meekly. She hated that she felt that way about him. Still. She hated him for making her see that she was no different in death than she had been in life.

"And for that you took people's heads off, sliced their throats, shot them in the heart while their family watched, chased people down all the while hooting like some kind of crazy person. You did all that because you didn't want to lose me?"

Tara felt ashamed. True, she did a lot of it because of him. Most of it. But there was some part of her that liked it. People had to die, everyone did. She figured she was just helping some of them along.

"You bastard," Tara said under her breath.

"See," Mileeha said, standing from his chair to look at her. He looked the way he did the last time she saw him. He was Mitch again. His chocolate skin was smooth and beautiful, his shoulders broad and solid. She wanted to go to him, to let him hold her, to let him love her the way she remembered, but she forced herself to stand still.

"That's the difference between you and me," Mileeha continued. "I admitted the truth to myself. I knew I liked killing the first time I saw my father do it. I peaked through the keyhole and watched while he killed hookers, wanting to be in there doing the same thing. When I killed the first time, I didn't run away crying the way you did. I stood up tall and looked at my handy work. To me it was like artwork, something to be admired, something to be proud of. That's why I was surprised to end up here. I never hid the fact that I liked what I was doing. I wore it like a banner.

"But you," he said as he walked toward her. His eyes were deep and dark. Beautiful and frightening in their intensity. She was lost in them. "You couldn't admit it, even to yourself. But you know I'm right. You liked killing just as much as I did. And you should have been in Hell right alongside me."

Mileeha was close enough to smack, but she couldn't bring herself to do it. He was right. He was always right.

Mileeha smiled. Tara was as beautiful as he remembered her to be. She came in angry but even then, the anger was waning. She couldn't resist him, never could. She was like his little puppet. He never manipulated her, never took her for granted. She had him as much as he had her.

Mileeha wanted to take her when they got to The Realm but knew he couldn't. He had to gain a position on his own if he was going to stay there. Then he could bring her in. So, he waited. Bided his time. He ingratiated himself with Mal, working him, showing his loyalty for years. And the hard work paid off. Mal offered him a big chunk of the pie. All the Hunters were his; they obeyed his every command. He decided who would be converted and who would be eaten. He dispatched them to pick up the condemned. He had cart blanche. Until Patrick came along. Then he had to do things the way Mal wanted them done. Patrick couldn't be used as bait, nor could he be eaten. Not that it mattered to Mileeha, but he didn't like being told what to do. People who did that had ended up seeing the business end of a pistol. When he was alive.

But now Tara was ready. The anger was gone and she could love him again. He could make a good home for her one that looked however she wanted it to. Mal wouldn't like it at first, but then again, he wouldn't be there that long. Tara would be his second in command when he took Mal's place.

There was so much he wanted to share with her.

"Think of it as me saving you from an eternity of torment. Really, I *saved* your life," he continued.

Mileeha touched Tara's cheek. She turned her head. He touched her again, first with only a finger, then with his whole hand.

His hand felt so warm against her skin.

"I never thought I'd feel your touch again," she whispered.

"We can be like this for eternity. You and me here, in this house. We can make it look any way you want it would just be us. The Hunters would never bother us, no one would. It would just be you and me. Forever."

Tara fell into the fantasy. She heard the spear clatter the floor, but the sound was far away. She could see them enjoying each other again, being together anywhere they wanted. They could try to figure out how to get out of the Great Nothingness together. The Watchers wouldn't have to run and hide. They would be protected if Tara asked. She was starting to believe, starting to want it.

Mileeha's arms engulfed her as they had so many times before. She laid her head on his chest and let him hold her, his warmth mingling with hers. She wanted to stay there forever. Just like he said.

"It would be you and me again. Everything in The Realm would be ours."

As inviting as it all sounded, something about the picture didn't seem right. It nagged at her, that little detail, until she could no longer remain silent. Tara didn't want to ruin the moment, but she had to know.

"What about Mal? Where is he in all of this?"

Mileeha leaned in to Tara, cupping his lips over her ear. He hadn't been that close to her in longer than he cared to remember. A tingle shot through his body.

He whispered one word. "Gone."

Tara pulled back, missing his lips as soon as they were gone. "What do you mean?" she asked louder than she should have.

"This will be ours. All ours. I haven't figured out how to do it yet, but I will make it happen."

Tara pulled away from the embrace reluctantly. Was he talking about doing what she thought he was? Killing Mal? It couldn't be done. As far as she knew, Mal was like Satan and God - He just was. There was no story of how he came to be. He was always there. A former mortal couldn't kill him. She doubted if anything could.

Tara was speaking before she had formed cognizant thought. "It can't be done! It just can't be done!" Her voice was shrill, panicked. She didn't want to think about what the punishment might be for trying to kill Mal. It might be better to be in Hell.

"It can be done and I'm going to do it, but I want you by my side when I do." He looked at Tara meaningfully. Tara recoiled even further. To her, his eyes had glazed over, had become the eyes of a rabid animal.

Tara wrenched herself free of his grasp and took a step toward the door. "You're not making any sense," she screeched. "Do you know what he can do to you?"

"What can be worse than this? What, is he going to kill me again? I've been through it enough times to know it's never as bad as the first time. What else? Send me to Hell? I've got family there." Mileeha closed the gap between him and Tara. "We can do this, Tara."

Tara shook her head slowly, almost imperceptibly. She wanted to leave The Realm, not run it. She wasn't as content with her lot in life as Mileeha seemed to be. He enjoyed The Realm, wanted to stay. And why wouldn't he? He hadn't struggled the way she had. He never had to run from Hunters.

"Tara, I want you to be my second in command."

Tara's mouth was open before she knew what she was going to say. "I can't. I won't."

CHAPTER SIXTY-ONE

"Kill her."

Patrick felt like he had been smacked out of a restful sleep. He turned to look around the room, instinctively searching for Doug. Doug was standing where he stood before. He was looking at him with same bleary-eyed confusion Patrick was sure was etched on his own face.

Mal was sitting where he had been before, his eyes upturned to Patrick as they had been before. Mal had been talking about something, the details of which Patrick couldn't remember. He wondered if Doug did, but was afraid to ask in front of Mal. Mal's voice was rising, falling, sounding more and more muffled, like he was holding gauze over his mouth as he spoke. And then two words came through as clearly as if he had said them himself.

Kill her.

Mal was smiling, his teeth sharp little points in blood red gums.

CHAPTER SIXTY-TWO

Mal's voice filled Mileeha's head like the beating of a drum. It blocked out all other thoughts and replaced them with only his voice, his command. Mileeha had never felt Mal's presence in his mind before; he never knew Mal could find his way in. His own skills came from a family line of soothsayers. He took for granted that he was the only one who knew how to do it, and allowed himself to get careless, cocky. It was a mistake that would cost him everything.

Kill her, Mileeha.

No, Mileeha spat at the voice in his head. He felt vulnerable, open. He was enraged. *I will not kill her.*

You would choose her over me? I gave you a position of authority, let you control the very beasts that would rip you to shreds if I wish it. I put them, and the whole of The Realm, under your thumb. And you would betray me for a woman.

It's not for a woman that I do this, Mileeha hissed. He could feel Mal's grip tightening in his mind, choking him as though his hand was on his throat. Mal was going to kill him and Mileeha knew it. And there was nothing he could do to stop him. He could see Tara through the narrow slits left open by his clinched eyelids. She was pressed against the door as she had been before, staring at him with wide eyes. She wasn't grabbing him, asking what was wrong, trying to still his convulsing body. She was just standing there. Staring. In that moment he wondered why he had been so blind. She was weak. She could never have taken on the responsibilities he would have expected her to perform.

In his last show of power, Mileeha sent a message to the Hunters. He told them to kill. Kill everyone in sight.

CHAPTER SIXTY-THREE

Patrick and Doug sat in front of Mal as he watched the scenario in the other room play out, hoping they looked calm. They were anything but. Mal might have been distracted, but he was still aware of them.

Patrick asked, after a period of uncomfortable silence, "Do you know who my relatives are? The ones that are here because of me?"

Mal turned his attention to Patrick and snickered before answering. "I'm sure they'll make themselves known to you the moment you take the position."

Patrick's stomach dropped. That was the last thing he needed: an angry mob of people wanting to exact revenge on him for sending them to The Realm. They would try to hurt him, kill him if they could. The ones who had been there the longest were the ones to be most afraid of. They knew there was no way out of The Realm. They would want his head.

Mal studied Patrick's eyes, waiting for him to falter. He didn't, but not because he didn't want to. He was too afraid to show weakness in front of Mal for Doug's sake.

It was a test, Patrick knew. One that he would be expected to pass, or he and Doug might be killed just as quickly as they had come into power. Patrick tried to make his face look as confident as he could. He returned Mal's gaze.

Mal replied with rich, jubilant laughter.

CHAPTER SIXTY-FOUR

It was like a switch kicked over and turned the lights on. The Hunters' eyes seemed to brighten; a brilliant green radiated from them like a glowing light.

Sebastian, Kincaid, Aadi, Qiao, and Lydjauk were between the house and the Hunters. They were just about to go inside, to help Tara with what must certainly have been a suicide mission, when one of the Hunters moaned like a dying animal. The sound jarred them. They bumped into each other, almost dropping their weapons. As they watched, the Hunters seemed to stretch, their spiny backs rippling beneath the gelatinous membrane that covered them. Their tentacles writhed wildly, as if searching the air, scouring it, enjoying the smell of fear. The Hunters flexed their hands, the suctions opening and closing as though gulping air. One of them turned toward Sebastian, sized him up, and bent his legs like it was preparing to spring.

The Hunters were awake. And they were hungry.

CHAPTER SIXTY-FIVE

Mal squeezed tighter, constricting Mileeha's airway.

Do you feel your chest closing, your lungs burning? It hurts just like it was when you were alive, doesn't it?

Mal was enjoying Mileeha's pain and he reflected it in his voice. Mileeha tried to block him, tried to use everything he had ever learned from his family to push him out of his head, but nothing worked. He would have been surprised if it had.

This is my air, my neck, my body, Mal hissed. The sound reverberated in Mileeha's head, bouncing off the walls and echoing on top of itself. It sounded like an agitated rattlesnake. I allowed you to use it when I could have let you run around in the broken body you died in. Or in nothing at all. I control The Realm. You never could have.

Mileeha gasped for air as Mal squeezed, his thoughts a jumbled mess of hatred and disappointment. Mal had been reading his mind from the start. He had been watching, waiting for him to develop a plan, waiting for him to utter the deceitful words into the air.

Mileeha's eyes, bulging painfully now, rested on Tara once again. She was still standing there, watching him suffer. She didn't run. She just stood there as though frozen in fear. It was the same way she used to act, through all of their lives together - nothing changed. She was as much a coward now as she was then, and he felt the same old feeling creeping up from the pit of his stomach. He hated himself for loving her.

Could she have been involved in Mal's plan to kill him or did she just happened to be the person to hear his wretched disloyalty? Mileeha didn't know. All he knew for certain was that, just as in their final life together, she was going to die with him. He would see to it.

"Get out," Mileeha whispered, affecting concern. "Leave while you still can."

Tara seemed to wake up after hearing his words. Before then everything was muted; there was no sound, no image other than Mileeha's tortured face and squeaky gasps. Tara turned toward the door and, casting once last look at Mileeha over her shoulder, left the house. Her spear lay on the floor near Mileeha's twitching legs. As Tara ran out of the house and into waiting arms of hungry Hunters, Mileeha took his last breath. The sound of her scream raised a smiled of pure joy on his dying face.

CHAPTER SIXTY-SIX

When Tara left the house, her eyes were filled with tears. She wanted to be with Mileeha, had always wanted to, she could admit that now. But his plan was impossible. Mal would never have let that happen. He didn't allow Mileeha time enough to explain his plan, let alone act on it. If he would do that to his own son, she could only imagine what he would have done to her.

She had watched Mileeha die. Again.

Tara felt defeated. Worn out. She had sacrificed her friends and hurt a man who cared about her enough to chase after something that wasn't even real, something that wouldn't have ever been possible, no matter how much they wanted it to be. And now it was all over. She was all alone.

Tara lifted her head and looked at the trees that led to the woods. She was trying to decide which way to go. She couldn't go back to The Watcher's camp, not yet. She was too ashamed. Even if she could face the rest of them, she couldn't face Sebastian. She had hurt him too

deeply. She thought she might make camp on the hillside opposite The
Watchers camp. Maybe by morning she would have summoned enough
guts to go back. To go home. With any luck, they might take her back.

Before she could take her first step, she noticed the blood on
the ground. She hunched down, dropping to her knees, and crawled,
trying to keep out of sight. Tattered clothing was strewn around the
ground between the house and the well where she had hidden before.
There was blood everywhere. Tara looked toward the clearing where
the Hunters had been before. She thought she saw something lying
in the dirt, something she wished she hadn't seen. Tara cried into her
hand, gripping her mouth tightly as she did, cursing the scream that
had already escaped her lips. She laid her other hand down to balance
herself and ran across something sharp. She cradled Sebastian's knife
in her arms like it was a baby.

After everything that happened, The Watchers — her friends —
had come after her. They tried to help her. And the Hunters got them.

It was all her fault. Their deaths, like so many others, were on her
head.

A groan sounded in the distance, like a zombie awaking for the
first time. Tara froze. She no longer felt like she could overcome them.
Something was different. Tara hadn't been afraid of a Hunter since her
first couple of weeks in The Realm. They had been nothing more than
animals to her. But that confidence was gone. She saw them as she had
those first nights, their toothy, salivating jaws seemed to yearn for her
skin.

She suddenly felt naked. Her spear was inside the house on the
floor. With Mileeha.

Tara tried the door, but it was locked. She pressed her back against
it and peered into the darkness, her eyes scanning wildly. At first, she
didn't see anything. She wondered if her mind had been playing tricks
on her. Then, from the far side of what she thought might have been

a barn in another time, in another world, she saw two of them coming slowly, their jaws working hungrily.

Tara ran.

She held onto Sebastian's knife for dear life as she pumped her arms and legs up the incline and into the woods. The Hunters gave chase a lot faster than they ever had, grunting and growling behind her from the effort. Tara realized what had really happed with brutal clarity. It was Mileeha all along. He made the Hunters leave them alone. That was why they were able to kill them with such ease. It was all part of his plan to take down Mal. Who else would be so easily manipulated, so easily handled? Who else was already behind the eight ball because she loved him?

He had been playing her from the start. Even when they were alive, he had been buttering her up for whatever he wanted her to do. He wanted her to come to the house, wanted her to join him in his ridiculous plan. And when she said no, he turned the Hunters on her; only her friends had gotten in the way. It was as clear to her as words printed on a page now, but it was too late. She had fallen for it, had done whatever he wanted, and had ended up there, in The Realm, running for her life with her friends warming the Hunters bellies. She didn't know how Hell could have been much worse.

Tara ran with everything she had, suffering the low branches that cut her face and the rocks that jutted out to slice the bottoms of her feet. She ran through the woods remembering her childhood, imagining that she was behind her uncle's house, carefree and happy on a beautiful summer day. She ran because it was the only thing she knew how to do.

CHAPTER SIXTY-SEVEN

"It's yours if you want it," Mal said with the confidence of an employer offering a high paying job to an applicant. He was giving Patrick and Doug an opportunity they couldn't refuse.

"And Mileeha?" Doug asked. His throat was dry and he felt antsy. Something about the whole thing wasn't right. Things were going too well.

"It's already been taken care of," Mal said, his eyes twinkling deviously. Patrick found his eyes being drawn to the door that led to the kitchen.

"You'll do things the way I want them, but I don't make many demands," Mal said, his lips spread in a wide grin. He looked somehow familiar, like a face in an old picture.

"The Hunters will be yours, as well as this house. You have to dispatch Hunters to get the people whose names are in my book. Once they're dead, you're finished."

Patrick listened with a detached ear. Something about Mal was changing. Morphing. He looked more and more like someone he knew. Just when he thought he could put his finger on it, his face changed to something else. Patrick was staring at him, unable to pull his eyes away. He wondered if Doug saw the same thing.

"That's all?" Patrick heard Doug asking. "That's all you want from us?" He glanced at his Dad out of the corner of his eye.

"Is there something else you want to do?" Mal was amused. Doug was going to be fun. He would question his father when the evening was over and they were relaxing on real furniture for the first time since their deaths. He would want to know why this happened so fast, without out a fuss. Patrick wouldn't be able to answer him. Mal was sure of that; he could already see confusion clouding over Patrick's eyes. He would be just as confused as Doug was. And that was good. Mal wanted them lost. It would make it easier to get what he wanted out of them.

"Is there some other role you'd like to play?"

Doug didn't have an answer for Mal's question. It wasn't like he was really interested in the inner workings of The Realm. He was hoping that he and his father could figure out a way to save Gabby and themselves. Maybe God hadn't turned his back on his father yet. Maybe there was still a chance for them to get out of there.

Patrick was mesmerized by Mal's face. He could hear Doug speaking and heard the answers Mal gave, but the words were unimportant to him. Mal's face was changing, moving, teasing him with visages that were hauntingly familiar. At one point he thought he saw an old-time stage actor's countenance looking back at him, his face done up in thick, over-dramatized makeup. Patrick remembered he and his father seeing a sidewalk show starring the man whose visage flickered in front of him. Before Patrick could grab onto it, the face was gone.

Mal's face melted into that of the paperboy that used to ride his parent's route. Patrick knew the kid, had gone to school with him. He was older than Patrick by maybe two years, but when they saw each other at recess the older kid always said hello. Bobby. Bobby Caldwell, that was his name.

As Patrick watched Mal's face changed many times after that, merging features, brown eyes, blond hair, brown skin, green eyes, blue eyes, wide nose, cleft chin, black hair. Patrick blinked, trying to sort the images as they permeated his mind, jumbling, shifting, switching.

Patrick thought he saw he saw his own face in one of the jumbles of features, streaked with blood.

He gasped and jerked his head toward Doug. His eyes were wide, his jaw slack. He wanted to reach out for his son, he wanted to feel his arm beneath his hand, he wanted — needed — to stabilize himself, but he couldn't move.

Doug asked if he was all right and Patrick didn't know if he answered. He turned to look at Mal again, afraid of what he might see, but knowing he had to look. His cautious glance was met with a brilliant smile, full of teeth as sharp as knives.

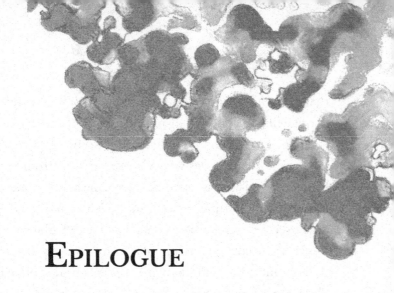

EPILOGUE

The room she was in was not one she had ever seen before. Hardwood panels adorned the walls and the floor was a dark, lined tile. There were no windows and no doors. It was as if she had gotten there by walking through a wall, a wall that had abruptly sealed back up as soon as she was inside. It was as small as a closet. She had been there for more years than she could count.

She heard no voices, though she knew people were in the house. There was a presence, some sort of thickening of the air when people were near. She read somewhere that animals could tell when bad people were coming by the way the air smelled. She thought she had developed that talent too, after being by herself in silence for so long.

No one came to see her except a man that looked like her first boyfriend in high school. The first time she saw him she was happy – how bad could a place be if it brought fond memories? She asked him if he was Charlie, but he didn't answer. He only smiled the same smile that made her go out with him in the first place. It tickled her, made her feel like a schoolgirl again.

He came often in the beginning, seeming to appear out of nowhere while her eyes were closed. He went from smiling to speaking by his third visit. His voice was the same as she remembered. They talked about old times – well, she did most of the talking. Charlie didn't seem to remember as much as she did. She started to wonder if maybe she was imagining him, calling him up from the recesses of her mind to sit with her while she was held captive in that strange place. She asked him if he was real. He just laughed at her. The laughter sounded cold.

Charlie didn't come much anymore and that was just as well. She was starting not like him anymore. She started to wonder what she was doing there and where she was. Surely, she wasn't in heaven. Heaven was supposed to be beautiful. She was supposed to see her family, all of them waiting for her as soon as she came through the pearly gates. She was supposed to match babies with mothers and answer her great-grandchildren's questions. She wasn't experiencing anything – no joy, no pain. So, where was she?

Purgatory?

She didn't even believe in such a place. She always thought it was made-up a sort of limbo for people who hoped to still get into Heaven on a second try. Just because you don't believe in something doesn't mean it isn't real.

She leaned against the wall and slid down to rest her bottom against her heels. She wasn't afraid – the time for fear had long passed. She wondered if she was going crazy and that drew tears from her eyes. Throughout her illness she worried about that. It was one of the things her doctors told her could happen with terminally ill patients. She fought hard to keep her wits about her, to keep a stiff upper life, and, in the end, to get her affairs in order. To lose her mind now, after the suffering was supposed to be over, was a bitter injustice if she had ever heard of one. She couldn't stop the tears from coming. They dripped onto cheeks that were as gaunt and pale as they were when she died. Joanne didn't wipe them away.

L. Marie Wood is an award-winning author and screenwriter.

She is the recipient of the Golden Stake Award for her novel *The Promise Keeper* and the Harold L. Brown Award for her screenplay *Home Party*. Her short story, "The Ever After" is part of the Bram Stoker Award Finalist anthology *Sycorax's Daughters*. Wood was recognized in *The Mammoth Book of Best New Horror, Vol. 15* and as one of the 100+ Black Women in Horror Fiction.

Active in the horror community, Wood is an officer in Diverse Writers and Artists of Speculative Fiction (DWASF).

To learn more about L. Marie Wood, visit her website www.lmariewood.com.

Coming Soon
Book 2 in The Realm Series

THE REALM: CACAPHONY

Toddlers and playdates and white picket fences. Afternoons in the park, steak on the grill - all in the perfect neighborhood. Gabby was living a life that many people could only wish for and she was over it. It wasn't that she disliked her world - it wasn't that at all...she loved her family and the life that she and her husband had made. She just wanted more - more action, more stimulation, more excitement.

Gabby was bored.

But while she spent her days washing sand out of hair and making PB&J sandwiches, a battle was going on in The Realm, a cosmic tug of war over the most inimitable of prizes: Gabby's very soul.

Coming Soon from L. Marie Wood

THE PROMISE KEEPER

A young girl, on the cusp of sexual maturity, in what is now known as Benin, West Africa, is seduced by a beautiful stranger, a man the likes of which she has never seen before. Their encounter changes her forever. She becomes an *asiman*, a vampire: one of the undead.

The Promise Keeper comes to her, willing her to do his bidding – to keep an unspoken promise. He probes her mind and plants suggestions so she will follow his plan, until she fights back. She runs, her travels taking her to Europe and the Caribbean over centuries to escape him. She finally settles in New York City, convinced that she has eluded him… until she falls in love.

The Promise Keeper is a story of love, despair, murder, and deceit. It is also a vampire tale like no other.

More from Cedar Grove Publishing

OBSIDIAN TALES
BOOK 1

Sadie Abdullah • Pat Canterbury • Geraldine Hunter
Raphael Jackson • Rae James • Valjeanne Jeffers
Nann Mahon • Kimberly Wiley • L. Marie Wood
Edited by Boranda Diaz

More from Cedar Grove Publishing

Sycorax's Daughters

Edited by Kinitra Brooks, PhD.
Linda D. Addison & Susana Morris, PhD.
Foreword by Walidah Imarisha